Outstanding praise for R.J. Stevens and her debut novel
BECOMING BOBBIE

"Bobbie's sincere and good humored approach makes
for a highly engaging tale. It's a love story, but it's also
a story about being true to yourself. It's hard not to
like Bobbie's unflinching honesty and appealing lack
of pretense . . . through Stevens's warm and engaging
account, the sums of its parts add up to something
much greater."
—*The Lambda Book Report*

"Stevens's debut novel is exquisitely nuanced. The use
of a first-person narrative voice preordains a happy-
ever-after ending, but that predictability doesn't dimin-
ish at all the pitch-perfect tone of Bobbie's emotional
downs, ups and eventual even keel."
—*The Front Page*

Books by R.J. Stevens

BECOMING BOBBIE

THE BEST OF FRIENDS

Published by Kensington Publishing Corporation

The Best of Friends

R.J. Stevens

KENSINGTON BOOKS
http://www.kensingtonbooks.com

KENSINGTON BOOKS are published by

Kensington Publishing Corp.
850 Third Avenue
New York, NY 10022

All Kensington titles, imprints and distributed lines are available at special quantity discounts for bulk purchases for sales promotion, premiums, fund-raising, educational or institutional use.

Special book excerpts or customized printings can also be created to fit specific needs. For details, write or phone the office of the Kensington Special Sales Manager: Kensington Publishing Corp., 850 Third Avenue, New York, NY 10022. Attn. Special Sales Department. Phone: 1-800-221-2647.

Kensington and the K logo Reg. U.S. Pat. & TM Off.

ISBN 0-7582-0849-9

First Kensington Trade Paperback Printing: April 2005
10 9 8 7 6 5 4 3 2 1

Printed in the United States of America

For Kody
Heroism is all in the heart.

Acknowledgments

Emergency Services is exactly that; a service. And I have had the honor to serve with so many, from volunteers to paid professionals, and I thank each and every one of them for their dedication and inspiration. While the characters in this story are fictional, I hope I have made their respective professions proud.

Terrie, you are, as always, my constant.

Chapter One

Shelby Tucker gazed through the windshield as her partner, Bryce Johnson, drove the ambulance at a breakneck speed. Bryce casually reached over and turned up the volume of his favorite classic rock station, his huge hands making the radio knob look ridiculously small as his strong baritone voice joined The Eagles, singing about someone having a "Heartache Tonight."

The double-shutter flashes of the blue strobe light on the front fender made still pictures of the ditch beside the road. From the corner of her eye Shelby could see a whole world in that ditch, the individual blades of grass standing out in sharp relief against the blackness of the night, each one with a perfectly detailed shadow stretching out behind it. The raindrops from the light mist seemed to freeze in midair, standing still in time as they flew by. She saw the occasional small animal whose life was interrupted by their passing, frozen in fear from the noise and lights, or a quick flash as they ran away.

Shelby saw the world in the ditch, in still flashes, but her mind stayed in her world, sharp and focused. Her eyes registered the flashing of the light bar on top of the ambulance, reflecting its colors into the night. Up-down, up-down, blue-red, blue-red, the colors swept across her view. Her eyes saw the flashes of color washing across her vision, but her mind only registered them as on, unaffected by their hypnotic rhythm as she watched the road ahead.

A car wreck on a night like this, and me without my rain gear. I should have seen it coming.

She reached down without looking and selected an extra large pair of gloves from the boxes between the seats, laying them on Bryce's leg with a quick double pat. He gave one nod to acknowledge them, never taking his eyes off the road ahead or missing a word of the song. Shelby selected a smaller pair for herself, pulling them on and swaying slightly in her seat as Bryce screamed around a corner. Someone else driving at this speed, in this weather, would have made her nervous, but not Bryce. She trusted the big man to handle the ambulance under any conditions and to know when to slow down.

They saw the flashing glow over the next hill and Bryce began to slow down. As he pulled the ambulance up behind a police cruiser, Shelby's trained eyes swept around the area. The skid marks quickly fading from the wet asphalt and the debris in the road told her an all too familiar story. The car had been heading north when the driver had lost control, hitting a signpost before spinning and rocketing into the deep ditch on the southbound side.

The flashing lights lit up the night, reflecting off the raindrops and broken glass, making shadows jump long and short, turning the scene before her first blue, then eerily red. Shelby turned her head and looked through the side window without noticing that she looked through her own thin reflection, the ghostly image of her own face, pale and small in the darkness, the hazel eyes transparently staring into hers as she looked down into the ditch.

She saw the car, a late-model Camaro, the front end smashed against a tree. The driver's door was open; there was an officer Shelby didn't recognize standing next to it, and a man with him, holding his own arm at an awkward angle.

She recognized the second officer, even from behind, leaning in the passenger side of the car, holding the head of the person inside.

Shelby took in all of this in a matter of seconds as Bryce parked the unit and she keyed the mike on the two-way radio, telling Dispatch they were on scene. She grabbed the trauma bag and climbed out, glancing at Bryce. He headed for the officer standing with the driver of the car, and she went toward the other officer.

The drizzling rain soaked Shelby through almost immediately, plastering her medium-length hair to her face and neck, darkening her gray uniform and making it cling to her body. When she stepped close enough, she reached out and put her hand on the officer's back and leaned over her shoulder, tiptoeing slightly to see over her. Her voice was low and rough, even though she spoke softly.

"I see you've got yourself a new partner, Tori."

Officer Tori Pataki grunted assent and leaned to one side, giving Shelby a better view of her patient.

"It's a J-nasty, Shel. Class-one head; I can't keep him conscious."

Shelby noticed how Tori held the man's head immobile while pressing a blood-soaked bandage to his head in the hairline above his left eye. It was an awkward position for Tori, and Shelby quickly pulled fresh wound coverings from her trauma bag. She reached around Tori and pressed them on top of the first, freeing Tori's hand to better hold the man's head. She spoke up a little, her smoky voice commanding attention.

"Hey, buddy, can you hear me?"

The man groaned.

"Is he trapped in there, Tori?"

Tori shook her head, raindrops scattering from the plastic-covered brim of her hat. "Don't think so, just couldn't get him out by myself."

Shelby heard the sound of approaching footsteps and looked up to see the other officer and Bryce heading her way. She jerked her head quickly to one side, tossing the wet hair out of her eyes.

"Driver, Bry?"

Bryce jerked a thumb toward the officer and drawled casually, "He's in custody, maybe got a broken arm, but won't let me touch him."

"We're here for you, darlin'." Shelby spoke confidently, her rough voice as calm as if she were doing nothing more exciting than reciting a laundry list, while she reached around Tori with her other hand and began feeling her patient's face and head.

"Class-one head, rapid extrication. Anybody know his name?"

The officers shook their heads. Bryce grabbed the officer he was with and took off toward the ambulance. Shelby softly whistled as she noted the starred windshield and the loose-hanging seat belt.

Unrestrained, his head hit the windshield, knees into the dash, check for femur and hip fractures, maybe chest injury from the dash.

She quickly felt the man's pulse and ran her hand down his chest, looking for injuries. The man was young, maybe in his early twenties, and he was groggy, almost unconscious, his breathing slow and shallow. Shelby carefully placed her fingers between Tori's splayed ones and took over holding his head immobilized while she spoke to him.

"Hey, buddy, can you hear me?"

There was no response.

As soon as Shelby's hands were in place, Tori slid hers

out and went around the car, climbing in from the other side and sliding all the way over, positioning herself in the backseat behind the injured man. When Tori took his head again, Shelby pulled a roll of gauze out of her bag and wrapped it around the man's head to hold the bloody bandage in place and free up her own hands while talking to him the whole time.

"Okay, buddy, we're going to get you out of here. Just hold on for me."

She forced open the door and reached down to the man's feet as he groaned again.

"I'm going to get rid of some of this stuff on you now. Don't fight me, buddy. Let me do my job, all right?"

Shelby grasped the cuff of his jeans in one hand and started cutting them off, her purple-handled trauma shears slicing quickly and easily through his jeans. She moved with surety and confidence, her scissors working their way up along his body and her face remaining impassive as her mind calculated all the possible injuries the man could have.

Bryce and the other officer came over with the cot, backboard, C-collar, and straps. Bryce leaned over Shelby and put the stiff collar around the man's neck, fastening down the Velcro. Shelby threw a quick look at the other officer standing as if he wasn't sure what to do, and her wet hair fell back into her eyes.

"You." Her voice wasn't overly loud, but it commanded attention. She glanced at his name tag. "Reid?"

He nodded.

"You ever assist an extrication before, Reid?"

He shook his head.

She again tossed her hair out of her eyes with a jerk of her head. "Okay, what we're going to do is put him on that board, flat on his back, without moving his spine.

We'll move him a little bit at a time. What we need from you is to hold that end of the board steady while we put him on it. Got it?"

Officer Reid nodded.

"Okay, buddy, here we go."

"Billy." Officer Reid spoke up for the first time. "His friend says his name is Billy."

Shelby nodded and began using the name, explaining to him again what they were going to do to him. Bryce positioned one end of the board against the man's leg, put Officer Reid at the other end and showed him how he wanted the board held in place. Shelby didn't seem to notice the board in her way as she ran her gloved hands quickly over her patient's nearly naked body, whistling softly to herself as her hands worked and her mind noted and filed away every abnormality.

From her viewpoint over the man's shoulder, Tori watched Shelby work. Her strong hands were large in comparison to her small stature, and they moved over the man deftly, flexible and sure, as if they had a mind of their own and were able to see and correct any injuries the man might have. Tori smiled.

Maybe they can. If anyone can, it's Shel. Does she know how funny it sounds for her to be whistling an upbeat tune in the middle of all this mess? Does she even realize that she's whistling? Probably not.

Satisfied she had found all the serious injuries, Shelby stepped back and went around the car, absently brushing broken glass out of her way as she crawled in and knelt on the driver's seat.

"All right, I've got his legs, looks like a possible femur fracture on the left. Bryce, take the torso, we'll turn him on three. Tori, on your count."

"Okay. It'll take two turns; the doorpost is in my way. Everybody ready?" She glanced at their placement and continued. "One . . . two . . . three." They moved the man smoothly, Bryce and Tori turning his head and body together, Shelby lifting and straightening his legs as they went, until Tori's right arm came in contact with the doorpost of the car.

"That's it, I've got to move. Bryce?"

Bryce took the man's head, Shelby continued to whistle and held her position as Tori clambered over her back to get out of the car. She went around to the other side of the car and took over the man's head from the outside. Bryce squeezed himself into the floorboard and slid his hands into position on the torso. Tori checked their positions and they turned him when she counted again.

"One . . . two . . . three. He's there."

Without a word they shifted again, Bryce standing up outside the car to take control of the man's shoulders, quickly checking his bare back for injuries, Shelby climbing over the console and taking hold of his hips. Tori glanced at them to make sure they were in position.

"Let's go up. One, and two, and slide." Tori stepped backward as they moved him, until she brushed against her partner. "Perfect."

Officer Reid held the board steady while the other three quickly strapped the man down and taped his head in place on the board. They lifted him to the cot and wheeled it up the bank to the ambulance. Bryce didn't seem to notice that he'd brushed Officer Reid aside as they loaded the cot.

Tori jumped in and began setting up an IV as Bryce dropped into the captain's seat, turned on the oxygen and began to breathe for the man with a bag-valve-mask. Shelby readied the intubation equipment.

Bryce lifted the mask off the patient's face and leaned over as far as he could in his seat, dropping his left leg straight, allowing Shelby space to work. She resumed her low whistle, changing the tune to match the radio, faintly heard through the opening between the cab and the back of the ambulance. She dropped to her knees above the patient's head, held the tube in her right hand, rested her right elbow on Bryce's knee, and inserted the laryngoscope deep into the man's throat with her left hand.

Lifting the laryngoscope, still whistling, Shelby peered in. As she slid the tube into place, her right elbow slid down her partner's left leg.

"Oooh, baby, do it again."

Bryce grinned as he made his comment, his hands automatically yanking his equipment apart and attaching the bag directly to the tube, dropping the mask on the floor beside his seat.

"I'd love to, but I'm all done," Shelby teased back without breaking stride. She stood and leaned over his hands, listening to the man's lungs with her stethoscope as Bryce squeezed the bag.

Tori, one hand on Shelby's back, roll of tape in the other, stepped around her. Shelby nodded and slid to her left, picking the needle out of the package that Tori had opened for her. Tori inflated the bulb on the end of the tube in the man's throat and taped it in place before tearing several varying sized strips of tape, sticking them on the bar above Shelby's head. Bryce continued to squeeze the bag rhythmically, his baritone voice joining Shelby's whistle, softly singing along with Peter Frampton.

Shelby cleaned her IV site and pulled the cap off the needle with her teeth. "Okay, Billy, big stick here." Her unconscious whistling turned into a low hum as she threaded the needle into a vein in his arm. As soon as she got a flash of blood, Tori handed her the IV tubing and jumped out the side door of the ambulance, making her way to the open back doors and standing next to her partner.

Shelby hooked the tubing to the catheter, casually dropping the needle in the sharps container and opening up the flow valve. She reached above her head and took the strips of tape without looking, taped the catheter in place and yanked the rubber tourniquet off with a snap.

Bryce stepped out the side door, running around the front of the unit and getting in the driver's seat. Shelby took over squeezing the bag and spit the needle cap into the trash can with a quick glance at her watch and a grin at the officers.

"Eleven minutes. Great job, guys, thanks."

Tori grinned back, shut the back doors and slapped them twice, signaling to Bryce that he was clear to go. As they sped away, she turned to her partner.

"Your first extrication assist, huh?"

He nodded.

She clapped him on the back. "You did a fine job."

"Do you think he'll live?"

She shrugged. "I don't know, he's in pretty bad shape. He's damn lucky he didn't go through that windshield and into that tree. But he's got the best crew in the county working on him. If anybody can get him there in time, it's Shelby and Bryce."

Officer Reid eyed his partner suspiciously. "You know her?"

"Know her?" Tori laughed, shaking the water from her plastic-covered patrol hat. "Yeah, I guess you could say that. Come on, let's get this guy checked out so we can take him in."

"We should just take him in anyway. When he wakes up in the morning hurting like hell, maybe he'll learn a lesson."

Tori looked at him, her eyebrows raised in surprise.

"I'm just kidding! I wouldn't really do that."

"Well, I might." She laughed as she climbed in the passenger side of the cruiser. "But policy is policy."

Officer Reid looked at his partner and smiled as he headed the car toward the hospital.

They arrived shortly after the ambulance and took their prisoner into the emergency room. The hospital security guard temporarily took over custody of the prisoner, so the officers thanked him and went outside to wait.

They stepped through the sliding doors of the ER and found themselves at the back of an ambulance. The back doors were flung open and the sound of rock and roll was wafting out. Bryce jumped out the doors and beat a perfect drum solo tattoo in the air with imaginary sticks before taking Tori off her feet in a bear hug.

"Hey, girlfriend! Good to work with you again!" He jerked a thumb at her partner. "Who's the new guy?"

Tori laughed and hugged him back. "This is my new partner, Ryan Reid. Ryan, this is my friend, and a damn good EMT, Bryce Johnson."

Bryce turned and looked at Ryan, keeping his left arm around Tori. Although she was broad-shouldered and medium height, five and a half feet or so, Bryce's arm engulfed her. He was a large man, standing well over six feet, his shoulders spanning the width of most doorways. His light hair was receding at his temples and long enough to rest on his collar. His size would have made him look formidable if not for the slight paunch hanging over his belt and his disarming smile. His light brown eyes assessed Ryan critically.

Ryan looked back impassively with his blue eyes. His face held a chiseled beauty beneath his perfectly tanned skin, and his emotions were held carefully in check. He was as tall as Bryce, though his body was leaner and more disciplined. His blond hair was cut in a severe military style and his uniform was perfectly creased. They shook hands and exchanged wary hellos, then Bryce turned back to Tori.

"So, are you gonna keep this one?" His deep voice drawled the question out, and Tori caught the glint of humor in his eye.

She slipped her arm around her friend and looked at her partner appreciatively. "I hope so, I kind of like him." She gave Bryce a squeeze. "I've got to go back in, be nice to him, will you?"

Bryce winked at her. "I'll try."

Tori went back inside and headed for the bathroom. She walked with long, confident strides, arms swinging with her elbows slightly bent to avoid her gun belt. Her eyes moved constantly, taking in everything around her. Years of law enforcement had her trained to always be on the lookout for everything.

A passing nurse waved at her as she opened the bathroom door. Tori turned her head to smile and wave back as she stepped in, her vigilance momentarily broken.

What the . . . ? Tori's heart skipped a beat as someone suddenly grabbed her and pushed her back against the bathroom door, pushing the door shut and pinning her hands above her head as a body pressed close and a low voice whispered against her neck.

"Hey, Cop, you ever made it in a public bathroom before?"

The voice wasn't just deep and rough now, it was raspy, guttural, and Tori knew it well. She also knew the contours of the body pressed against hers. Before she could answer the question, her mouth was covered with a hard kiss.

Tori kissed back, tilting her head and leaning in hungrily. When the kiss broke, she grinned slyly.

"No, I've never made it in a public bathroom, but I'd like to!"

Shelby let go of Tori's hands, threw her head back and laughed. Tori smiled, watching her laugh.

No one had ever accused Shelby Tucker of being drop-dead gorgeous. She would never be a model. Her features were what Tori considered average, a little better than plain, but nothing that immediately stood out and grabbed attention. At first glance her lips seemed a little thin, her nose perhaps a bit too long. Fine lines were beginning to show around her eyes and mouth, and she was starting to look just a little tired. She had an edge to her face that seemed somehow hard.

Oh, but when she laughs . . .

Shelby's laugh reached every part of her face. Her hazel eyes sparkled, the odd flecks of brown and green shining with happiness. Her mouth opened wide, as if her laugh was something huge that came from somewhere deep within, and her mouth couldn't hold it all. Those fine lines were lost in creases of joy, and to Tori her small features were transformed into the most beautiful face on earth.

She's radiant.

Tori touched her lover's damp hair hanging in loose, chunky layers just past her shoulders. The sandy color was darkened to a light brown by the rain, making it look shaggy and unkempt.

The same way it looks when she's sweating, she thought with a bigger smile. *"Fuck me hair," she calls it.* She batted her eyes coyly.

"So, are you going to make love to me in the bathroom, or what?"

Tori stood almost four inches taller, and Shelby had to look up into her eyes. Her dark hair was in a neat French braid that hung down between her shoulder blades; the light made it shine like midnight silk. Her dark skin tone was a contrast to Shelby's own, and her eyes were a sea green. Those eyes had captured Shelby's heart the first time she had seen them, little pools of ocean mist looking out from that dark, heart-shaped gypsy face, and she could still look into them forever. There was nothing in the world she wanted more than to make love to her right then. She reached up and gently touched Tori's face, her heart feeling as if it was swelling inside her chest.

"I love you . . ."

"But you've got to go," Tori finished for her and smiled. "I know. I have to go, too. But I'll be home in . . . oh," she glanced at her watch, "about two hours. You'll be waiting for me?"

Shelby turned with a grin. "I'll be the one naked in your bed."

Tori laughed and gave her a playful push. "You're such a slut."

"Thanks, you taught me well." Shelby gave her a wink as she slipped out to find her partner.

Bryce was waiting for Shelby in the ambulance, drumming a beat on the dash. She climbed in behind the wheel. He turned down the music, looked at her and grinned.

"So, how was your bathroom encounter? Did you get any on ya?"

Shelby laughed and slapped his arm playfully. "I can't get anything past you, can I?"

"Nope!"

The dispatcher's voice blared over the scanner. "EMS Seventeen, priority one, one-thirty-two Old Mill Road. Fall, hip pain."

Shelby copied the call by radio, flipped on the emergency lights and glanced over at Bryce as he cranked up the radio and they both sang along.

Shelby laughed out loud. *Bryce is the coolest straight man on the face of the earth and he's my partner.* "God, I *love* my job!" She slapped the wheel and laughed again as they sped into the night, still singing along to the radio, the siren wailing above it all.

Tori came out of the bathroom to find Ryan waiting by the door for her. He tipped his head toward the emergency room, where an orderly was pushing a bed with their prisoner on it toward the elevator.

"He's got a broken arm, and they want to keep him overnight for observation or something. They're taking him up to the secure ward. I finished the paperwork, all I need is your signature and we're set."

Tori nodded. "He's upped a class due to the severity of the injury to another person in the same vehicle. They'll hand him over in the morning. Any word on the other guy?"

"They think he's going to make it."

She nodded again. "Good."

Ryan gave her a strange look, but didn't say anything as she signed the paperwork and they climbed back into the patrol car. Tori drove through the drizzling rain in silence for a while. She glanced at Ryan from time to time, always catching him hurriedly looking away.

What's with him? Have I done something? Did Bryce say something?

"How did Bryce treat you?"

Ryan shrugged. "Seems like a nice enough guy."

Tori waited for something else from her partner and got nothing.

"Are you okay with the wreck tonight? Your first with real injuries, wasn't it?"

"Yeah, I'm cool."

Are you, really? "You know, we could talk about it if you want, it's okay."

"No, I'm cool, really."

Ryan turned his face to the window and stared out into the night. Tori continued driving until she could bear his silence no longer. She pulled the car into an empty lot where they could see the highway, turned on the radar gun and shifted in her seat so that she could look directly at him.

"All right, Partner, what's up?"

Ryan shrugged innocently. "Nothing. It's just that . . . I didn't know . . ." He stumbled over his own words, looking for the right way to express himself. "Well, you . . . no. Umm . . ." He stopped, shook his head and took a deep breath. "You did a really good job with that guy at the wreck tonight. You looked like you've done that a lot."

"Well, I have."

Tori grinned at Ryan's surprise. "I'm a licensed Emergency Medical Technician. I have been for about nine years."

"Oh." Ryan looked out his window a moment, then back at her. "I thought you'd been on the force longer than that."

"I have." *Where's he going with this?* "I'd been on the force for a couple of years when I took the EMT training."

"Why? I mean, weren't you happy with Law Enforcement?"

"Oh, yeah. I just wanted to do more. You know, you work so many accidents, sometimes you're the only one there for a while. You just want to be able to . . . *do* something, you know?"

"It wasn't because they gave you a hard time on the job? I mean, I've heard that it's harder for . . ." He looked down at his hands. "Harder for women."

Tori narrowed her eyes to slits, watching her partner. *Harder for women? You ought to try being a lesbian!* "It can be. I do okay, though."

"Oh."

Tori sighed. "So I wanted the training. And when I found out the department would pay for it, I couldn't pass it up."

Ryan spoke quietly, still refusing to meet her gaze. "And is that where you met her?"

"Shelby? Yes." Tori smiled. "She was my instructor."

Ryan turned his face to the window again, watching the rain run down the glass. "And how long was it before she was your lover?"

So that's where this is going. No wonder he acts so nervous. Tori looked at him, irritated. His face was a blank mask; she couldn't tell if he was trying to provoke her. But she liked him, and wanted to be honest with him. *Damn it, I don't want to lose another partner because of this. Why does this always come up? Shelby doesn't have a problem with it.* She sighed, knowing she'd be honest, regardless of the consequences. She gazed out the window, taking her mind back to meeting Shelby.

Ryan watched Tori as she stared out the window. He could see her irritation in the way she held her jaw, tight and stern. He watched her irritation turn into something else, something nostalgic, and maybe a little sad. He wanted to reach over and touch her arm, tell her it was all right. As he lifted his hand to do just that, she began to speak.

"We were friends instantly." She spoke quietly, closing her eyes. The last ten years melted away in her mind and she could almost smell the classroom, almost see Shelby standing there, her back to her, reaching up to write on the dry-erase board. "I was barely on time. I walked into that class just as she was starting to introduce herself. She was standing at the front of the room, writing her name and a great big number one on the board. I sneaked in and slipped into an empty seat, hoping she wouldn't notice. She turned around and looked me dead in the eyes. I thought she was going to say something to me about being late. She didn't, just looked at me a minute, then gave me the slightest little smile, barely a smile at all, but she was looking at me. I felt like she could see right through me. In that split second, we became friends."

Tori opened her eyes, looking out the window at the passing cars, not really seeing them, seeing instead the first memories of her lover. "She was just so open, so real. There was no bullshit with Shelby, still isn't. She was so out there, so free. I wanted that." She sighed, pulling herself back to the present and glancing at Ryan. He was looking at her expectantly, so she continued.

"I guess I had a crush on her right from the start. I'd had brief encounters with other women, nothing serious. But the moment I saw her, I just . . . fell." She smiled, her mind sliding easily back in time again.

"I used to call her up with questions about class. She always invited me down to the ambulance base to help me, and even to her house a couple of times. I really didn't need help, and I guess she knew that. But she helped me anyway. I did everything I could just to be near her.

"I tried to take it further once. I knew she was a lesbian. Hell, everybody knew. Shelby's never kept that a secret. Nobody knew about me, but she found out quick. We were at her house, and she was helping me with patient assessments. That's very 'hands on,' and you touch the person almost everywhere. She was on the floor. I was feeling over her body for 'injuries.' I couldn't help myself. I tried to kiss her."

Tori flushed a little, hoping it was too dark for Ryan to see. "She was so tactful about the whole thing. She sat me down and explained that she would love to be my friend, but she would never date a student. Shel somehow manages to turn you down without making you feel like a total jerk. The day the state board results came in, she called me to tell me that I had passed. And she asked me out. I don't think I ever went home from that date."

Tori sat silent for a moment; then she shook herself out of her memories and hardened her jaw.

"We did nothing wrong or unethical. I won't apologize to you or anyone else for who I am. I am a professional at work and what I do off duty is my business. If you have a problem with that, we can get you reassigned to another partner."

She looked at Ryan and suddenly realized that he was laughing. He laughed almost silently, his shoulders shaking and tears streaming from his eyes. He wiped at the tears and tried to bring himself under control.

Tori's voice betrayed her growing anger. "Something funny?"

Ryan shook his head. "No." He giggled. "You just sound so defensive."

Tori's anger flashed. *Why can't everyone let this alone?* "I've caught a lot of shit over this. It's hard enough to be a cop as a woman, much less as a lesbian."

"Well, that explains the locker room incident."

"What?" Tori hated being confused, it always made her angry. She was angry enough without confusion compounding it.

"Yesterday, when I was assigned to you, I was changing into my uniform when the guys in the locker room started razzing me about how I looked like a 'real man' and maybe I could 'set you right.'"

He was giggling uncontrollably. Tori had never heard a man giggle like that before. If she could have let go of her anger, she would have been astonished. But she couldn't let it go, it flashed into fury.

"And you find that funny?"

"Yeah." He giggled. "I do. And you would, too."

"I don't think so. In fact . . ."

Ryan interrupted her with another giggle.

"Tori, honey, I'm gay."

Chapter Two

Shelby parked her car in the driveway and quietly un-locked the front door. She moved through the front room easily in the early dawn light, and continued up the stairs. Turning left at the top, she slipped into the first bed-room. The thirteen-year-old boy was sleeping peacefully. Shelby watched him sleep for a moment before she gently kissed his forehead.

He'd hate it if he knew I do that. He's getting so old, too old for Mom to tuck in anymore.

Shelby slipped from that room, crossed the hall, and entered the next. She pulled the covers back up to the ten-year-old girl's chin and brushed the hair off her face before moving back into the hall. She entered the room at the end of the hall, noticing the vast difference between the twin beds.

One bed was set askew to the wall, the covers all kicked to the floor. She picked them up and covered the eldest of the twins, kissing her softly and knowing the covers would be back on the floor before the sun finished coming up.

Shelby stepped to the second bed, neatly placed a few inches from the wall, covers pulled primly up to the sleep-ing girl's chest. She leaned over and the child held her arms out to her. Shelby smiled. In all of her twelve years, Erica had never failed to wake up when she came to tuck her in. Shelby whispered a goodnight and slipped out of the room.

Passing the stairs and going to her own room on the right of the hall, Shelby stepped into soft candlelight. Tori was lying on top of the covers, waiting for her. She sat down and stroked her lover's unbound hair. Tori reached up and took her hand.

"You're late, baby. I was just about to send out the cavalry. Bad call?"

Shelby nodded. Tori waited, knowing she would talk about it if she gave her enough time. Finally, she did.

"Eighteen-month-old. God, we worked so hard on him." She closed her eyes and shook her head. Tori waited for her to continue. Shelby leaned over and put her head on Tori's chest. Tori stroked her hair and listened.

"I just don't understand how someone can abuse another person, much less a child."

Tori closed her eyes, hating the thought that her lover had to see the evil in the world. "Beaten?"

"Shaken. He wouldn't stop crying. His mother shook him until he did. An hour and a half later." Tori felt Shelby's hot tears against her flesh. "He'll never cry again."

Tori wrapped her arms around Shelby and held her tightly. "Did you talk to Chris?"

"No. I'll be okay. I just . . . It hurts. You know."

"Yeah, I know." *I know all too well, my love.* "Did you tuck in the kids?"

Shelby sniffled and wiped her eyes. "Yeah."

"Good. Can I do anything?"

"You can thank God night rotation is over."

"I do. At least it's over until next month. But can I do anything for you?"

Shelby sat up, wiped her eyes and shook her head. "No. I just want a shower."

Tori watched Shelby go into the bathroom and waited until she heard the shower running. She knew what she could do. She got up and followed her lover.

Shelby was standing in the shower letting the hot water wash over her when she felt Tori's hands slide down her back. She allowed herself to get lost in her lover's hands as they continued to roam over her body. She pressed close. Shelby leaned her head back, resting it on Tori's shoulder. *She always knows what to do. No matter how bad it gets, my Tori always finds a way to reaffirm life to me.* She gave in to her lover's caress, letting her muscles relax and her body respond to the touch.

People would think we were sick if they knew. They would never understand.

Tori wrapped the fingers of her left hand in Shelby's hair, turned her head and kissed her passionately. All thoughts left Shelby's mind as she responded, turning around and circling her arms around her. Tori whispered softly. Shelby gazed into her eyes, and they stood there, making love, letting their love and the water wash away the pain, putting the long night behind them.

Laura stood behind the counter at the bookstore and looked around. The soft, earthy scent of the incense Hannah had burned that morning hung in the air, giving the whole place an almost magical feel. The books were neatly placed in sections, the spaces between filled with trinkets and tools of a celestial nature. *It feels like home. Just like Aunt Martha's house used to.*

The door opened with a tinkling of bells, and she walked in. She was a woman unlike any Laura had ever seen before. She moved with a grace that belied her size.

She was nearly six feet tall and Laura thought she could almost see her muscles ripple like a cat's under her snug black T-shirt. Her hair was the color of honey with the sunlight shining through it, and it fell in thick waves to the curve of her buttocks. Her legs were lean and long, covered in jeans that were well worn and faded to a blue so light they were almost white. Laura caught her breath, imagining how soft those faded jeans would feel with the hard-muscled legs beneath them.

Her black work boots were faded, scuffed, and well used. Her features were strong, with high cheek bones and a wide, square line to her jaw. She walked with a loose-hipped grace that made Laura envious.

She glanced toward Laura and lifted one eyebrow in a questioning arch as she walked by. *No, not walking, striding,* Laura thought. *She* strides, *with confidence, a purpose. Very no nonsense. She has a destination in mind.* She strode purposefully by, heading for the women's interest section. Laura jumped, realizing that she'd been staring. She heard a throat clear behind her and blushed as she spun around, her heart pounding in her ears. It was Hannah, with a stack of books in her arms.

"Laura, where do you want these filed, by subject or in 'new releases'?"

"Um, I don't know." Laura tried to cover the fact that she was trembling. "How about subject?"

"Okay." Hannah smiled to herself as she walked away.

Laura turned back around and cursed softly under her breath. Hannah made her nervous. She was a full-blood Sioux, and Laura just knew she had some sort of magic about her. Those obsidian eyes of hers seemed to look right through Laura's skin, and she just knew that Hannah knew things. Just knew, without being told. Like the way she had known Laura the first time they had met, and the way she was always behind her when she needed something. Not to mention what she did in that little back room, her *readings*.

Although Hannah's ebony hair showed only a few strands of silver, her face had a weathered look that told of a life outdoors. Laura couldn't imagine why a woman like Hannah wanted to keep working at a bookstore. But it had been a stipulation in Aunt Martha's will when she bequeathed the place to Laura. And Laura would never go against Aunt Martha's wishes.

But now Hannah had seen her watching that woman. That woman, who had come into the store with such an aura of power and strength about her. That woman, who had so easily captured her attention, almost commanded it.

She caught me up in her so fast, as easily as if . . .

Laura was jerked out of her thoughts by the very woman she was thinking about. She sauntered up to the counter with a book. Laura kept her eyes down when she punched the price into the cash register, afraid she'd stare again.

"Will that be all for you today?"

"No."

The woman's voice was as big and attention-grabbing as she was, and Laura jerked her head up at the sound of it. She found herself staring into the most beautiful blue eyes she had ever seen, deep and piercing. Her breath caught and her thoughts jumbled. She swam in those eyes a moment before she found her voice.

"What else can I do for you?"

The woman gave her a slow, flirtatious smile that made Laura catch her breath again. She leaned her elbows on the counter and watched Laura with her piercing eyes. "You're new here, aren't you?"

Laura nodded and swallowed hard.

"I didn't see any French Vanilla incense on the rack. Hannah usually holds back a couple packs for me." She tapped the counter with one long, slender finger. "You should be able to find them in a sack under the counter."

Laura looked and found the sack. There were two packs of incense in it; she took them out and added them to the price of the book before rebagging it all together.

"Is there anything else I can do for you, ma'am?"

The woman cocked an eyebrow and smiled slowly again. "I don't think so, but thank you."

Laura totaled the cost. The woman paid her, turned to leave, and then paused.

"Have you ever smelled French Vanilla incense before?"

Laura managed a smile. "I don't think so."

The woman opened one of the packs she had just bought and pulled out a stick. She produced a Zippo from her pocket. "Close your eyes."

Laura closed her eyes. The smell of vanilla filled her senses, making her feel light and airy, and somehow sensual. The woman's voice reached her ears, whispering, almost as if from a distance, "My name is Chris."

Laura opened her eyes. The stick of incense was sitting in a burner on the counter, and the woman was gone.

Chris walked out of the bookstore and around the corner before stopping and leaning against the wall of a building.

God, why did I do that? I was flirting with that girl, and she's not even my type. She's too . . . too . . . Hell, she's probably straight. She's way too young, even if she does look like . . . Chris, why can't you just leave it alone?

But she couldn't leave it alone. The girl in the bookstore had stirred something within her that she hadn't felt in a long time. It wasn't her looks. *Although,* Chris admitted to herself, *she is attractive. She's so small, even her face looked as if it would break if it was touched too hard. Delicate.*

Her light brown hair was cut short and tousled, and her skin was so light, so smooth. *But she can't be over twenty-five, if that old. Ah, but those eyes, those big brown eyes have such softness, such innocence . . .*

Chris shook her head. *Get it out of your head, Chris. She's too young for you. And too complicated. That's just what you don't need, more complications.*

She shook her head again and walked on, trying to get the girl in the bookstore off her mind, afraid she wouldn't be able to.

Chapter Three

Shelby opened her eyes to the morning light. Tori slept soundly, one arm thrown across Shelby's chest. Just as she was wondering what woke her, she heard a soft knock on the bedroom door. She eased herself out of bed, slipped on a robe, and opened the door.

Suddenly, a twelve-year-old girl was in her arms, crying. Her sleepy mind tried to catch up to the situation.

"Hey, hey, Sammy, what's wrong?"

"Randy." Sammy was sobbing uncontrollably. "He hates me, Mommy, he hates me!"

"Hush, hush, child." Shelby stroked her daughter's hair and stepped completely out of the bedroom, softly closing the door behind her. "Randy doesn't hate you, honey. How could he? You've been best friends since you were four. What could have happened to change that?"

Shelby carried the child down the stairs and into the den while she spoke, trying to calm her. She sat on the sofa and put Sammy in her lap, rocking her until her sobs diminished.

"You okay?"

Sammy sniffled and nodded.

"All right, then. Tell me what this is all about."

Sammy wiped her eyes. Her voice caught and her breathing hitched, but she managed to speak. "R-Randy told me he h-h-hated me and he never ever w-wanted to t-t-talk to me again."

"Why?"

Sammy shook her head, more tears spilling from her eyes. Shelby tried to make her voice soothing.

"Sammy, honey, I can't help you if I don't know what's wrong. Now, come on, talk to me."

Sammy took a deep, hitching breath. "Last week Randy t-t-told me that he liked Kylee, and he wanted to know wh-wh-who I like. He said if I didn't tell him, then we weren't f-friends anymore."

Shelby nodded. "I see. Now he's mad because you won't tell him."

"B-b-but I did! Now he hates me!" She flew into more sobs.

Shelby rubbed a hand over face. "Okay, you lost me."

"I th-thought he'd understand. B-but when I told him I liked A-An-Angie, he got really mad. I called him this morning, and he's still mad. He-he said he h-hates me!"

Shelby's mind caught up and everything became clear. *Oh, God, already? Does this have to happen so soon?* "Oh, Sammy. Oh, honey, I'm sorry."

She held her daughter close and rocked her while she cried. Her mind wandered. What would she say to her? What *could* she say?

I liked Angie . . .

The words echoed in Shelby's mind as the significance of that simple statement hit her like a blow. She held her child until her sobs eased, then put a hand on her chin and tilted it up, forcing Sammy to look at her face, her eyes searching the girl's red swollen ones.

"You know that I've never lied to you, and I won't start now. You know that I'm gay, I never hid that from you. But you should know that not everybody is cool with it. Some people just aren't."

"Why not?"

Shelby shook her head. "I don't know, baby. Just some people . . . like Mom Tori's last partner. Do you remember him? The one that got fired?"

Sammy nodded.

"Do you want to know why?"

Another nod.

"Well," she smoothed Sammy's hair back from her face, "he didn't like Mom Tori, and he gave her a hard time." *Hard time, that's an understatement, Shelby. He harassed her horribly. Should you tell Sammy that? No, not yet.* "He was mean to her just because she's gay. *No other reason.* Some people are going to be like that no matter what you do about it. It's not right, but that's the way it is." She sighed and watched her daughter's face as she spoke, watching her words impact the child. "If this is the life that you are going to live, you need to remember that. Sometimes people don't like you, and you won't care. But sometimes it's going to be people that you do care about. And it'll hurt." *A lot.* "That's just the way it is sometimes."

Sammy looked at her, confusion and pain in her eyes. "But why do people hate us? Is love wrong? You love Mom Tori, that's not wrong, is it?"

Us? My God, she's thought this through. Shelby sighed. *Love isn't wrong, child, just hard. So hard sometimes.* "No, love isn't wrong. Some people just don't understand *this kind* of love. And they're afraid of what they don't understand. When people are afraid, they get mad. Then they hate what they're afraid of."

"So Randy's afraid of me?"

Shelby smiled sadly at her. *Is it really that simple?* "I

think maybe he just doesn't understand. He'll either come around or he'll lose the best friend he ever had. That's a choice he has to make."

Sammy sniffled and wiped the last of her tears away. "Will you talk to him?"

Shelby shook her head. "No, you have to. He's your friend. And that's part of it. This time it's about you, not me. If you want people to understand, *you* have to make them understand."

Sammy nodded and hugged Shelby. "Okay, Mom. I'll go talk to him right now." She got up from Shelby's lap. Shelby pulled her back.

"Hey, I love you, you know."

"I know, Mom. I love you, too." Sammy hugged her before turning and running off.

Shelby watched her daughter run from the room and saw Tori standing in the doorway. Tori walked over and sat down beside her.

"World's Greatest Mom strikes again."

Shelby leaned her head back against the couch, rubbing her face with both hands and sighing deeply. "Not hardly. God, I wasn't ready for that."

Tori took her hand. "Come on, Shel, we've talked about this. We have four children, and an open-minded household. That's pretty good odds that one of them will be gay or bisexual."

"I know."

"And of course it's Sammy. We've known that was a possibility for years. You know she's leaned that way all her life. Remember her first day of school? She came home and announced that she was going to marry her teacher. Her best friend is a boy. She won't wear anything she can't climb a tree in. She wants to play football, ride a bike, and get dirty. For Christmas last year she asked for a skateboard and a *tie*. She's never shown one sign of being straight!"

"I know." She ran her fingers through her recently slept-on hair, making it stick out worse. "I guess I just wasn't ready to hear it. She's twelve, Tor, *twelve,* and already out. Do you know what she's going to go through in high school? God, when she said that, a huge part of me wanted to scream 'no' and a part of me wanted to . . . oh!"

Shelby slapped her forehead with the palm of one hand. "Oh, God! She just came out to me and I didn't give her anything positive. *Nothing at all!* Oh, no. Oh, God, no. How could I not give her anything positive? Oh, I hope I haven't screwed her up."

Tori put her arm around Shelby's shoulders and began smoothing her hair, making it lie back in place.

How is she so collected on the job, so together around the kids, and such a wreck the rest of the time? I think I'm forever putting her back together, but no one else ever sees that. She sighed. "Yes, I do know what she'll go through. And you didn't screw her up. It's okay. She knows how you feel. We've always told the kids that we love them no matter what choices they make. I hope that I would have handled it as well, had it been me. *You did fine.* And she'll *be* fine."

"You think?" Shelby looked at her worriedly.

"I know." Tori stopped fussing over her lover's hair and began to trace the line of her jaw. "Now, are we still going out tonight?"

Shelby grinned slyly, her composure back as if it had been snapped into place. "Unless you have better plans."

"No." She dropped her hands into her lap and rolled her eyes. "Get your mind out of the gutter. I just wanted to invite Ryan along."

"Ryan?"

"Yeah."

"Your partner, that Ryan?"

"Yes."

"He's gay? And out?"

"Yes and no." Tori lifted Shelby's hand in both of her own. "He's gay, but he only came out to me. You know how the guys in the department are. He just needs to get out and meet some people. I think you'll like him, Shel, he's really sweet and cool and . . ."

"Hey, hey, okay. You don't have to sell him to me. He's your partner, and if you like him, that's good enough. Now shut up and kiss me."

Tori obliged.

Hannah watched Laura watch the door. The late afternoon sun poured through the window, making a soft halo around the younger woman's tousled hair. She tried to keep busy, but her eyes roamed back to the door and her hands became idle.

She's been watching the door since yesterday. Waiting for Chris to come back. She has no idea how many young women hoped that one would come back. Would she believe me if I told her that they were always disappointed?

Hanna couldn't stand to watch Laura watch that door any longer. She stepped up behind her.

"Hey, Laura, you want to close up and go out to an early dinner?"

"I don't know . . ." Laura tried to look busy, but she was too distracted. She couldn't get her mind off the woman that had come in the day before. Chris. But she didn't want Hannah to know.

Hannah touched her arm. "Oh, come on, it'll be fun. There's not enough business today to pay for the electricity we're using. Martha and I used to sneak out early about once a month or so."

Laura smiled at the image of her aunt sneaking out of work early. That was exactly the sort of thing she would have done. *And just the sort of thing I wouldn't. God, I need to loosen up.*

Hannah grinned at her, her dark eyes sparkling. "Try it, you might like it. Besides, it'll do you some good."

Laura looked startled. "Are you reading my mind?"

Hannah winked at her. "I don't have to, you're an open book. Come on, just this once."

Laura glanced back toward the door and sighed. "Okay, maybe just this once."

Hannah grinned again. "Great! Martha and I always went to a little outdoor café down the street, you'll love it." She helped Laura lock up and took her to the café.

They made light conversation until the waitress brought their meals. Hannah knew Laura was nervous, and wanted to put her at ease. She decided the girl's aunt was the best subject to talk about.

"Martha talked about you a lot." She said it casually. "You were close."

Laura's eyes lit up at the mention of her aunt. "Yes, we were. I used to spend hours and hours at her house when I was little. My parents hated it. They said she was 'an eccentric old fool.' "

Hannah laughed. "Eccentric, yes, but she was far from a fool. She was one of the sharpest people I'd ever met." She shook her head and smiled. "What did you do in all those hours that your parents hated?"

"Oh, she would take me on nature walks, show me different herbs and plants. She taught me how to garden, how to fly a kite, all kinds of things. I loved her so much. I thought she was the coolest person in the world, that she knew everything. She talked about my family history all the time. She wanted me to know where I came from. I learned about all of the skeletons in my family's closet from her."

Hanna looked off and smiled, as if at a fond memory. "I can see her doing that."

Laura nodded. "My parents were kind of reserved, emotionally. But not Aunt Martha. She was so open, so . . . demonstrative. She did all those things that they never would. She told me she loved me every time we spoke, and she hugged me all the time." She smiled, thinking back to her childhood with her favorite aunt. "Sometimes I wonder if I loved her more than my own parents. I always wanted to be with her. I remember when she moved here; I must have cried for weeks. I told her I'd come live with her someday. I'd help her run the bookstore. I guess I didn't make it in time." She sighed, a heavy, tired sigh. "You must have been close to her, too. She wrote about you in her last letter. I think she cared a lot about you."

Hannah smiled. "Yes, she did. And I cared about her, too. I thought for a while, years ago, that we'd be good together, but it didn't work. As special as she was to me, we decided we were better off as friends."

Laura stopped, fork halfway between her plate and her mouth. She stared at Hannah, unable to breathe for just a moment, her mind racing. "You weren't just friends?"

Hannah looked at her, realization suddenly catching up with her. *She didn't know. How could she not know? I'm sure I didn't read that wrong. She's been pining over Chris . . . Martha never mentioned that she was closeted with her. What else was she closeted about?* She blinked hard. "She never told you? I thought, since you were so close, that you knew."

"I didn't."

"We . . . we were, uh . . ."

Laura set her fork back down. "You were lovers." She made it sound almost like an accusation.

Hannah lifted her head proudly. "Yes, we were lovers."

Laura leaned forward and peered at the woman who had known a side of her beloved aunt that she had never dreamed existed. Hannah looked back at her calmly.

"You're shocked. I'm sorry. I didn't realize you didn't know. You were so close with Martha, I thought she would have told you."

"She didn't. She didn't tell me." Laura spoke softly, almost to herself. "Why wouldn't she tell me?"

Hannah raised her eyebrows. "Maybe she didn't think she needed to. Maybe she thought you knew."

Laura looked stricken. "Why would she think that? How would I know if she didn't tell me?"

"I don't know, maybe she just thought . . . Well, I thought . . ." she trailed off.

Laura looked at Hannah sharply. "You thought what?"

Hannah shifted in her seat, but kept her face impassive. "I just thought that you . . ."

"You thought I was gay, too?" Laura interrupted her.

"Well, yes. I saw the way you were looking at Chris, and I just . . ."

Chris. Suddenly, Laura was no longer defensive. Her lunch was forgotten. The conversation she was having was forgotten. Everything else flew from her mind at the mention of Chris. She put her elbows on the table, laced her fingers and leaned her chin on them, suddenly more interested than ever. "You know her?"

"Chris?" Hannah shrugged. "Of course I know her. Everybody knows Chris." *And why am I not warning her against* that *heartache? I should, but . . .* She shook the thought from her head. "So, are you?"

Laura furrowed her brow, confused. "Am I what?"

Hannah threw up her hands and rolled her eyes. "Gay!"

Laura sat back, tucking a stray strand of hair behind her ear. *Am I? All I can think about is this woman; does that make me gay? God, I don't know!* "Honestly, I don't know what I am. I don't think I know anything right now." *Have I ever known anything?*

She thought back, trying to find anything that would tell her. High school had been a lonely time. She had taken all the hardest classes, and kept to herself. She'd had a boyfriend in her senior year, but it hadn't felt like a real relationship to her. He was someone who took her to the dances, and an occasional movie, but they had never gone parking or made out. He didn't seem to want to.

College was a little better, she had more boyfriends, had even slept with two of them. *But something was wrong with me, because I never felt anything. No fireworks, not even sparks. And never that feeling I got looking at Chris.*

Hannah smiled and held her hand out to her. "Give me your hand."

Laura eyed her suspiciously, but gave Hannah her hand. Hannah studied the palm a moment before letting it go. Laura thought Hannah looked as if she knew something that Laura didn't. She looked down at her own palm.

"What, do I have some sort of gay line?"

Hannah laughed. "No such thing. I think you're a lovely young lady who's been stuck in a small town for so long that you haven't had a chance to find yourself."

Laura sighed, sitting back again and dropping her hands to her lap. *Does that make me gay? Feeling . . . something when I look at that woman, something that I never felt looking at a man? Or was it just* her? *I'll bet everyone wants her, gay or straight.* "Maybe. Maybe I'm just confused. I don't know."

"And that's okay. You weren't born with all the answers, you know. At least, not in this lifetime." Hannah grinned at her, and Laura couldn't help but smile back.

"This lifetime? Now you sound like Aunt Martha."

"Good, then I'm becoming one of the coolest people in the world." She took another bite before looking back at Laura. "Hey, you like to dance?"

Laura shrugged. "Sure."

"Why don't you come to the bar with me tonight?"

Laura tensed up, looking at Hannah closely. *What is she getting at?*

Hannah laughed again and shook her head. "Relax, honey. I'm not asking you out. Child, you are way, *way* too young for me. I just meant that you could come out with me. Dance a little, you know, cut loose. You can meet some people, maybe have a little fun for a change. I'll bet you haven't been out of your apartment except to go to the store or work since you've been here."

"No, I haven't," she admitted. "What kind of place is this you're taking me to?"

"So you'll go?"

Laura smiled, beginning to relax. "Sure, I'll go. What kind of place is it?"

Hannah shrugged. "It's a bar, honey. What do you mean?"

"I mean, like what kind of bar? What should I wear?"

"Anything you want," she said with a laugh. "Nothing looks out of place at Margie's."

Chris stopped in front of the closed bookstore. She stood there a moment, looking at the locked door. *Shut down early. It hasn't been closed early since Martha died. What could have happened?* She turned around at the sound of a wolf whistle. A man at a nearby construction site waved at her.

"Hey, baby! Why don't you come over here?"

Chris rolled her eyes and turned away. The man called to her again.

"Hey, baby, what's wrong? I'm trying to be friendly here."

Another man stepped up behind him. "Aw, don't worry about it man, there's other fish in the sea. Like that one!"

Chris heard another whistle and turned to see what the men were looking at. A woman stood not far from her, trying to light a cigarette. She was lovely, slim and pretty in her short, tight skirt and heels, her long black hair teased into tiny curls, fingernails painted deep red, her slender hands cupped around her matching red pout as she tried in vain to keep a flame on her lighter. She threw an exasperated look at the men calling to her.

Chris stepped over to her, pulled her Zippo out of her pocket and lit it. The woman stuck the end of her cigarette in the flame and sucked it to life. Blowing out smoke, she looked at Chris gratefully.

"Thanks, I thought I was going to have to resort to them." She tipped her head sideways to indicate the construction crew.

"Oh, you don't want to do that. It would just egg them on."

The woman rolled her eyes. "No shit. What's that all about anyway? All that yelling and whistling? I don't get it."

Chris smiled. "They just don't know any better. They need a quick lesson in how to treat a lady."

The woman batted her lashes and looked Chris up and down. "And I'll just bet you could give them one. I'm Sabrina." She held her hand out to Chris, but kept it close to her body, palm down. Chris smiled and took the proffered hand lightly in hers, lifting it to her face and bending slightly as she brushed her lips against it.

"Chris. It's a pleasure to meet you."

"Oh, the pleasure's all mine. Would you mind walking me past these wolves?"

"No problem, I'd love to."

Chris smiled at her and held her hand out to indicate that Sabrina should lead the way. She glanced back at the construction crew, now silent and sullen as they walked past, and grinned.

"*That,* gentlemen, is how to pick up a lady."

One of the guys waved a hand at her and turned away, the other one flipped her off. She heard him yell out "Dyke!" as she reached the corner of the street.

Just after they rounded the corner, out of sight of the construction crew, Sabrina stopped walking and looked at her. "Do you get that a lot?"

"What?"

She tipped her head back in the direction they had come. "*That.* The catcalls, the names."

Chris rolled her eyes again. "Oh, that." She shrugged. "Not too much, some people are just assholes. I've learned to ignore it."

"So are you? If you don't mind my asking."

"No, I don't mind, and yes, I am. I assume you're not."

Sabrina shook her head. "No." She looked Chris up and down appreciatively. "But I always wondered. And you might be enough to convince me. You wouldn't want to . . ."

Chris grinned. "I'm flattered. And usually, I would. But today . . . It's just not a good time for me."

Sabrina nodded and flicked her cigarette away. "I understand. Thanks for the light, and the escort."

Chris tipped her head in a mock bow. "Anytime, fair lady."

Sabrina reached into her purse and then held out her

hand again. Chris took it, finding that she was also taking a business card with it. Sabrina leaned close to her.

"If you change your mind, call me."

Chris nodded at her and slipped the card in her pocket as she watched her walk away, twitching beneath her skirt.

Now why didn't I take her up on that? It's not like me to turn that down. She watched Sabrina's legs appreciatively until she was out of sight. *I don't think I've ever turned down something like that before. There must be something wrong with me.*

Chapter Four

Laura tugged the T-shirt over her head and tossed it on the bed already strewn with discarded clothes. She pulled a dark blue sweater on and fluffed it around her jeans. She'd been at it nearly two hours, and still wasn't satisfied. She looked in the mirror, fussing over her hair.

It'll never do right, it never does. She caught herself and stopped. *God, Laura, what are you doing? Are you really trying to look good for tonight? Do you really want to?*

She heard a honk outside her window and looked out. Hannah waved up at her from the window of her little green Tracker. Laura waved back to let her know she had seen her, and took one more quick look in the mirror, hoping she didn't look as nervous as she felt, before grabbing her keys and running downstairs.

Laura marveled at the size of the bar when Hannah took her to a corner table. A massive L-shaped bar dominated one wall of the crowded room. She sat at the table Hannah took her to and watched in amazement. There were more people than she could count. People of every size, shape, and color.

This is so cool, all these different people together. How beautiful. And I'm here. But am I really a part of it all?

She watched the people around her. Her eye caught on a short woman, young and pretty, with her light brown hair teased and spiked in a careless style, talking to a woman even younger, with her blond ponytail hanging through the hole in the back of her baseball cap. The woman with the cap reached out and touched the other woman's arm in a universally flirtatious manner. Laura looked away quickly, only to find herself staring at another woman. This one was leaning on a rail, scoping the dance floor. With her belt and hat, Laura could easily picture her leaning in the same way on a fence, watching horses. Her eyes roamed farther into the room, settling on a large, dark-skinned woman. She was talking animatedly to an older woman who could have been of Latin or African-American descent. Laura couldn't tell in the lighting. *It doesn't matter, she's beautiful. They're all beautiful, from the oldest to the youngest, from the thin to the heavy. They are all beautiful.* Laura smiled sadly to herself, torn between the thrill of so many different people coming together, and feeling just a little on the outside. *But isn't that the way it's always been? I always wanted to be a sorority girl; I wanted that group of friends. Girls that I could stay up all night with, giggling and crying, eating ice cream and doing facials. But I never pledged. Why?*

But she knew why. She had been afraid. All her life, she had been afraid of not fitting in. She knew somehow that she wouldn't. After all, she didn't even fit in with her own family. Everyone else in her family was gregarious, her father a salesman, her mother in real estate, and both her brother and sister active and popular in school. They had all been confused when Laura, the youngest, showed signs of being introverted as young as five. As a child she found herself uncomfortable in her own home, wanting to hide from all the noise and commotion around her. She found solace and peace in the presence of her Aunt Martha, reveling in the quiet stillness of Martha's house, the slow and steady work of tending the garden, the gentle rocking of the porch swing, Martha holding her hand, not saying a word.

Hannah sat with Laura, trying to make sure she was okay. She watched her for any sign that she was more than just a little uncomfortable. *She's adapting well, perhaps she knows somewhere inside that this really is her element.*

Tori leaned in the window of the cab and paid the driver. As soon as Ryan opened the door, the bass beat began vibrating through them. They stepped into a small foyer with a door in the back corner and a desk. The man sitting behind the desk jumped up when he saw them. He ran around the desk and hugged them each in turn, talking so fast and flamboyantly that he was hard to understand.

"Girlfriends! Where have you been? I haven't seen you in so long! You both look so good! What have you . . . Oh, my God!" He stopped short and stared as his eyes landed on Ryan. "Who is this handsome devil? Oh my, please tell me he's friendly *and* single!"

Ryan's face reddened and the women laughed. Tori caught her breath and introduced them. "Jerry, this is Ryan, my new partner. Ryan, Jerry."

Ryan said hello and held out his hand. Jerry shook it with a flourish.

"Oooh, and he's a *cop*, too! Honey, I get off at midnight. You come arrest me just *any old time!* I'd love to see your handcuffs!"

Ryan laughed and Jerry buzzed the door open for them. Tori put her arm around Ryan as they walked through the door into a wide hallway.

"Don't worry, Jerry's an incorrigible flirt, but he really is harmless."

The hallway widened into a sitting area, with doors leading off to the right, left, and straight back. On the right was a small bar sparsely populated by women. There were men in the bar to the left. Tori led her party through the massive double doors in the back.

The room was huge. Through the door, directly on their left, was a large L-shaped bar. Shelby asked Ryan what he wanted to drink as they stepped over to it.

Just as the bartender was handing over their drinks, Ryan noticed a beautiful blonde walk up behind Shelby, put her arms around her and whisper in her ear. Shelby turned around and hugged her.

When Shelby let go of the woman, Tori stepped up and hugged her. "Hey, Chris, where have you been?"

Chris shrugged. "Here and there, you know."

"Well, it's good to see you. Shelby, we're going to go get a table. Chris, come sit with us when you two get done."

"I will." Chris gave Tori another hug before turning her attention back to Shelby. Tori grabbed her beer and steered Ryan through the crowd to a table close to the dance floor.

Ryan looked back at Shelby and Chris as they took their seats. "Who's that?"

Tori grinned. "That's Chris. I'm surprised you haven't met her yet. She looks pretty good, huh?"

Ryan whistled as he watched Chris. She had one ankle crossed over the other and was leaning one elbow on the bar, talking to Shelby. She looked relaxed, as if she belonged exactly where she was. As tall and broad as most men, she still gave off an air of femininity. She wore her firm, trim body like comfortable old clothes, and her faded jeans like a second skin. Her hair hung loose down her back, reaching the curve of her buttocks. And her face, with its symmetrical features, strong jaw and arched eyebrows, was open and friendly. Even in jeans and a T-shirt, she could have just stepped out of a fashion magazine.

"Damn! She's incredible! That's almost enough to make a guy change his mind! I can't believe you're leaving your woman alone with her."

Tori laughed. "Shelby and Chris go way back. I don't have any worries there. If they were any closer, they'd be sisters. They'll talk shop for a while, and then come find us."

Tori introduced Ryan to everyone she knew. He was amazed at the diverse group of people she called friends. There was Alex, a beautiful coffee-with-cream-colored woman who had strong opinions and the intelligence to back them up. And Margie, the heavyset blonde who owned the bar. She was in her late fifties and very soft-spoken. And there were men, all kinds of them, from leather-clad macho men to young pretty boys. But the one that Ryan noticed the most was David, a slight young man with dark skin and impeccable manners.

Before long, Ryan found himself dancing with David, having the time of his life. He found David to be sweet, effeminate and warm, if a little reserved. They were coming off the dance floor when David caught sight of Shelby, Chris, and a couple of other people making their way to the table.

"Ladies." He spoke with a slight English accent and kissed each one on the hand as he addressed them. "So glad you could join your party." He turned back to Ryan. "Thank you, Ryan, for the dance and the chat. I would like to dance with you again later, if you don't mind."

"I'd love to. Pull up a chair and join us."

"Oh, no sir. I'll leave you to visit with your friends a while, and join you later, if that's all right."

Ryan smiled, amused at David's reserved and proper manner. "I'd like that."

David stepped back and gave the slightest bow before turning around and walking away. Chris watched him go before turning to Ryan with a smile.

"David's quite taken with you." She held her hand out and he shook it. "You must be Tori's new partner. I'm Chris, and I'm very glad to meet you. Any friend of Tori and Shelby, you know."

"Ryan." He smiled at Chris and pulled out a chair for her. Chris inclined her head as she sat down.

"So, Ryan, tell me about yourself."

"Oh, there's not much to tell, really."

"No? That's hard to believe. I understand that you haven't been in Law Enforcement that long, but you're obviously not fresh out of high school, either." She eyed him critically a moment. "The hair and body says military, but you don't really have that walk. I'm sure there's more to you than meets the eye."

He laughed. "Maybe you should be a cop. You'd make a great detective."

Chris waved her hand. "Nah, I don't care much for the job description. But you're avoiding. Something you don't want to talk about?"

"Not at all." He waved a hand in dismissal and took a long swig of his beer. "I'm not military, but my father was. Career. I guess I followed in his footsteps more than I thought."

Chris drank her own beer. "But you didn't join up. Where have you been since high school? Nearly ten years, I'd guess."

"You'd guess about right. I was in college, mostly. Got

my bachelor's in criminology before I went into the academy."

"Ah, a cop to the core." She smiled sweetly to take away any possible sting in her words.

He shrugged. "I guess so. It's all I ever wanted to do."

Before he even realized it, Ryan was talking to Chris as if he'd known her all his life. He told her how he had always wanted to be a cop, even as a kid. He told her how hard it was to learn the job, even how heartbroken he was after the breakup of his last relationship. She listened, her blue eyes intense. She seemed wrapped up in everything he said, yet she was still able to add to the other conversations around the table. Ryan got the feeling she could make anyone feel like they were the only person in the room.

Chris listened to Ryan with interest, but her attention was wandering. She watched Tori and Shelby together, the way they laughed, the way they easily touched each other when they talked. *It must be amazing, that kind of intimacy, that kind of familiarity. How many years have they been together? Nine, ten? And yet Shel still looks at her like that, like she's the only thing in the world that matters. Is that possible?*

Tori said something that Chris didn't catch, but Shelby did. Shelby leaned over and put her hand on Tori's leg as she laughed. Chris shook the hair back from her face as she smiled at her friend, then her eyes wandered past Shelby and caught sight of a young woman sitting alone at a table.

Oh! It's her!

Chris had time to tip her beer at the young woman before Shelby sat up straight and blocked her view. She turned her attention back to Ryan.

Ryan finished his beer, and again a waitress brought him another. The waitress pointed to the bar, where David casually tipped his own drink toward him and smiled. Chris raised an eyebrow.

"David again. He's really taken with you. What'd you do to him?"

Ryan shook his head. "I didn't do anything. What's his story? Is he always this . . ." he glanced around, looking for the right words.

Chris offered him a questioning look. "Girlish?"

Ryan nodded. "I guess. He's kind of girlish, but not. Like . . . I don't know, like a bottom taking on a top role. Does that make sense?"

Chris shrugged. "Femmie-butch. Makes perfect sense to me."

Tori leaned over, speaking above the music. "David's a rich kid. He was born in a mansion on the right side of the tracks and basically raised by an English nanny. That's why he acts so proper. He's not putting on just because he likes you, he's really like that. I don't think it's so much girlish as it is just proper and . . . well, mannerly."

Ryan nodded. "Yeah, I guess that could be it."

As if he knew they were talking about him, David came strolling over to the table. "Mister Ryan, if these ladies have no objection, I would like the pleasure of your dance once again."

The women all wooed and whistled as Ryan was whisked away again, only to join him on the dance floor when the next song started. Except Chris, who went over to the bar, and then disappeared.

Laura sat watching a table near the dance floor. A group of about six or so people was gathered there, laughing and having a good time.

They look so comfortable; they're having so much fun. I wish I had that, a group of friends, people to have fun with, people who know me and accept me. I don't think

I've ever had that. Oh, but how I want it. Even to have one friend, someone to laugh with. There's been no one like that in my life except Aunt Martha.

As Laura watched, one of the women at the table moved and Laura inhaled sharply as Chris came into view. She was laughing, her head thrown back, her honey-colored hair waving. She looked over and tipped her beer toward Laura. Someone moved again, obliterating Laura's view. She sighed. Hannah touched her shoulder.

"Are you all right?"

"Oh, yeah, sure."

Hannah looked at her doubtfully. "You're sure? You look a little . . . homesick."

Laura laughed. "Homesick? No, not really. Unless it's possible to be homesick for something you've never had."

Hannah leaned in, looking intently at her. "Yes, that is possible. Just because you haven't had something this time around doesn't mean you can't miss it from the last time. The spirit's journey is long, and each road is different from the last."

Laura smiled. "You're sounding like Aunt Martha again."

"You were the daughter she never had. I'm sure there were things that she wanted to teach you and just didn't have the time."

"What kind of things?"

"Lessons of the spirit. I think she was setting you up for it when you were small."

"Really?"

Hannah smiled. "Did Martha ever do anything without a purpose?"

Laura shook her head. "I don't think so."

"Nor do I. I think she was teaching you more than you thought in all that time you spent with her. Nature was her church, and she was showing it to you."

Laura sighed. "I wish she would have finished. Maybe

I wouldn't feel so . . . out of place." She glanced at Hannah. "In my life."

"I think you could find your place, you just need to open up to it."

"You make it sound so easy."

"It is. I could teach you, if you want."

"You would do that for me?"

Hannah smiled at her. "I would be honored to take up where Martha left off. It's been a long time since I had a student, I think I'd enjoy it."

"I think I'd like that, if you're sure you don't mind."

Hannah pushed herself back from the table. "Great. Now, if you're okay, there's a lady who has been patiently awaiting my company."

Laura looked up and noticed an attractive black woman waiting a polite distance away. *Alex*, her mind supplied the name for her; she'd always been good with names. She smiled. "Yeah, sure, I'm fine. Have fun."

She rested her chin on her fist and watched Alex lead Hannah to the crowded dance floor. They joined the fray and were soon lost to Laura's view. Suddenly, she thought she caught the faint smell of vanilla and jerked her head up.

Chris was looking down at her, holding a drink. She set it on the table in front of Laura.

"Blue Kamikaze, right?"

She glanced at the glass, then back at Chris. "Yes. Would you like to sit down?"

"Yes, I would. But only if you agree to dance at least once with me."

She blushed a little. "Sure." She looked around nervously as Chris pulled out a chair and sat down. "Thanks for the drink; how'd you know?"

Chris leaned close and smiled. She knew she had enough charm to woo anyone, and she turned it on now, giving her full attention to Laura. "Would you believe I paid the bartender to tell me?"

"You did not!"

She grinned and arched one perfectly sculpted eyebrow. "You don't think? How else would I know?" She waved a hand and shrugged one shoulder. "The bartender's a pushover. She'll tell you anything for the right price."

Laura laughed, not sure if Chris was joking or not. "Well, thank you, Chris."

"I'm sorry, I don't know your name."

"Laura."

"Laura." Chris almost breathed the name, feeling it on her lips, closing her eyes and savoring it before continuing. "So, how long have you been working at the bookstore, Laura?"

"Just a couple of weeks. Do you go there a lot?"

Chris nodded. "I used to. I just haven't had much time lately. Work and stuff, you know, I don't have time to go as much as I'd like."

Laura nodded and picked up her drink. "I understand that. Where do you work?"

"The fire department."

Laura almost choked on her drink. "You're a fireman?"

Chris laughed. "Not really. I fight fires." She leaned back in her chair and spread her arms wide, palms up. Her snug T-shirt outlined her breasts, and her hair waved as she shook her head with a sly smile. "But I'm not a man."

Laura turned red and covered her face. "I see that . . . I mean, I'm sorry. I really didn't mean . . . I meant . . . uh . . ."

Chris was still laughing. "I know. Really, it's all right, I get that all the time. Say, do you want to go somewhere a little quieter?"

Laura looked around uncomfortably. "Well, I don't know . . ."

"Don't worry, Laura." She reached over and touched the back of her hand with one finger, making Laura inhale sharply. "I don't plan on stealing you away. There are two more bars in this building. I promise to be a perfect *gentleman*." She looked at the dance floor and pointed. "Hannah would kick my ass if I wasn't."

Laura blushed again. "All right."

They stood up and Chris put her hand against the small of Laura's back as they walked toward the door. Laura felt tingling excitement when Chris touched her. They went out the door and turned left, going through an open doorway. The second room was much smaller, with a few game tables and a jukebox in one corner. As Chris led her to a small booth near the jukebox, Laura noticed that only a few women were in this bar, and no men at all. They sat down. Laura sipped her drink nervously, trying to build up the courage to speak.

"So, do you like the bookstore?" She hoped that didn't sound as stupid to Chris as it did to her.

Chris smiled, watching the younger woman, enjoying her nervousness. "Yes, I do. I was really sorry to hear about Martha passing away. I guess you wouldn't know her, since you haven't been there long. She was a wonderful lady."

"Actually, I did know her. She was my aunt."

"Oh." Chris sounded a little uncomfortable. "I'm sorry."

"Don't be. Like you said, she was a wonderful lady, and I was privileged to know her for many years. At least I thought I did."

Chris raised an eyebrow questioningly.

Laura rolled her eyes. "Martha never told me she was gay."

"And that bothers you."

She sighed. "I guess it does. I just wish she would have told me. I could have, I don't know . . ."

"Connected somehow?"

Laura shrugged. "I guess. I just never thought of her that way. I never thought of her sexuality. She was my *aunt*."

"She was also a woman, Laura."

"I know." She sighed. "I just thought I knew her. And now I feel like I didn't."

"I think you did. Her sexuality was only a small part of who she was. Maybe she didn't think it was important enough to talk about. Or maybe she was waiting for the right time to tell you."

"Maybe. I hadn't thought of it that way, that she considered it a small part of who she was. I thought if you were gay, that was who you were."

Chris laughed. "Maybe it is for some people. Not for me. Defining yourself by your sexuality is like defining yourself by your job. It's a part of you, but not who you are. A person is so much more than that."

"I guess so." She shrugged. "Anyway."

Chris took Laura's hint and changed the subject. "So I guess you're running the store now?"

"I own it."

"It must be great, being your own boss."

"Not as much as you'd think. There's a lot of work involved. Hannah helps out a lot. Sometimes I wonder if she's the boss."

Chris leaned close. "I don't know what you believe in, but trust Hannah. Even if she says something that doesn't make sense, trust that she knows . . . whatever it is she needs to know."

Laura furrowed her brow. "I kind of got that feeling." She contemplated that a moment, and then changed the subject. "Tell me about your job. I don't think I've ever talked to a fireman, I mean a fire . . ." she paused.

"Fighter," Chris supplied with a half smile.

She nodded. "Firefighter, yeah. It must be exciting, saving lives and everything. You're a hero."

Chris shrugged. "People say that now, after nine-eleven. But I was a firefighter for a long time before that, and I'll be here long after the hype is all gone. It's just what I do." She took a deep breath, shaking off the melancholy that always gripped her when she thought about that day. "It's not all excitement, but I can't imagine doing anything else. It gets into you somehow, becomes a part of you."

"I'll bet it does."

"After a while it seems like you can't function in the real world for more than two days at a time. It's weird."

Laura looked at her, not understanding. "Two days? Why?"

Chris shrugged. "The shifts. We work twenty-four hours on, forty-eight off. So after two days in the real world, it's time to go back to work. After a while that's so natural to you"—she shrugged again—"nothing else seems right."

"Wow. And I thought a ten-hour day was rough! You must be exhausted all the time."

"Nah, not really. The station is really like a big house. We get to eat, sleep, and watch TV, whatever. It's kind of our home away from home. The crew gets to be like another family. It's as if I go home to my dozen or so brothers every couple of days. Just another home for us."

"I see. I guess we could all use another one of those."

"And it's not so bad, working ten days a month. Well, except for the months with thirty-one days, then we split the extra shift, just eight hours. I can't really complain."

Laura raised her eyebrows. "Ten days a month. Wow."

Chris looked at her and smiled, smoothly changing the conversation. "I didn't expect to see you here."

Laura shrugged. "I didn't really expect to be here.

Hannah brought me. She says I need to get out, meet some people."

"She's probably right. Hannah usually is. So, tell me about you, Laura."

Laura found herself relaxing and talking. Chris made her feel as if she was the only woman in the room, perhaps the only woman in the world. For the first time since Martha died, Laura felt comfortable talking to someone.

Before she realized it, hours had gone by. Hannah found them and asked if Laura was ready to go. She wasn't, but thought she should. She touched Chris's hand as she said good-bye, wishing she had the courage to kiss her. She didn't, but she did ask for her phone number, and got it.

As soon as Laura was out the door, another woman eyed Chris, vying for her attention. Chris automatically got another beer and sat next to the woman, whose blue eyes and knowledgeable hands found Chris irresistible. But Chris's mind kept wandering back to Laura, and her eyes kept finding their way back to the door.

Chapter Five

Chris automatically reached over and turned off her pager alarm as she opened her eyes. She paused a moment, seeing her own dim reflection in the mirror that hung over the big four-poster bed. In the predawn light she could just make out the form of the woman sprawled half across her. Slim and young, the woman was quite lovely. For just a moment, Chris allowed herself to imagine . . .

Her mind saw the woman—Brittany? Bethany? Barbie? She couldn't remember—change. Her cheeks filled out, making the bones there less prominent, her pouty lips thinned just a bit, making her nose look less turned up. The bare breast pressed against her side shrank, and the baby-fine hair shortened and darkened, becoming a light brown, tousled from a night of lovemaking. She looked at the reflection and saw herself smile, lying next to Laura.

She groaned under her breath. *What the hell are you doing, Chris? This isn't Laura, it's . . . Bethany. Brittany. Whatever. She's not Laura, and that's good. Get her out of your head.* She shook off the image and carefully eased out from under the woman. She gathered her things quietly, quickly dressing as she headed for the door.

Chris mounted her motorcycle and rode crazily into

the fire station. Tom, the off-going assistant chief, met her at the door with a grin.

"Rough night, Chris?"

She grunted at him and went upstairs to the living quarters, quickly showering and dressing in the spare uniform she always kept in her locker. As she bound her hair into a single braid she could hear the off-going crew slamming lockers and gathering their personal effects as they left and the fresh crew took over the space. She tied a bandanna snugly over the top of her head and wiped at the circles under her eyes.

Satisfied that she was ready for anything, Chris made her way into the kitchen, put on a pot of coffee and began making breakfast. She had done little more than gather ingredients when her chief came in, several fire-fighters trailing behind. He stepped up and rapped the counter. Chris set a cup of coffee in front of him.

"I know I missed roll call this morning, Chief, sorry about that."

The big man waved his hand at her. "We knew you were here. I came in to let you know I'm putting you on double duty today. We've got a new man; I'm putting him with you on Rescue and Attack."

Chris shrugged. "No problem. Where is he?"

A man stepped forward, solid and stocky, flashing a white smile and holding out his hand. "Hi, I'm Will."

Chris reached out and shook his hand. "Hey, Will." She looked back to the chief. "Are you stealing them out of high school nowadays, Chief? This guy *can't* be legal."

Will ran a hand through his curly black hair. "Actually, I am. I have two years experience in firefighting and I've even . . ."

"All right, all right, Will," the chief interrupted. "I'm sure Adams doesn't mean anything negative, do you, Adams?"

Chris grinned. "Nah, I don't mean anything by it. Just messing with the FNG, that's all."

"FNG?" Will looked at her.

Jimmy, a short, thin man with a shock of red hair and a sprinkling of freckles across his prominent nose, enthusiastically stepped up behind Will and put his hand on his shoulder. "Fuckin' New Guy. That was me until you came along. Elvis there is just giving you a rough time. You'll get used to it."

"Elvis?" He looked incredulously at her light hair and trim body with its obviously feminine curves.

Mark stepped up and leaned his elbows on the counter, his long blond hair falling in his eyes as he piped in. "Yeah, she's our very own hunk of burnin' love. And she's making breakfast, a sure sign that she didn't get home last night. Must have been a wild one, huh, Elvis?"

Chris chose several eggs out of the refrigerator and pushed the door shut with her foot. "Something you wouldn't know anything about, Pepe."

Mark's face turned red as the guys guffawed at Chris's return jibe. Jimmy grinned and explained to Will, "Pepe Le Pew, always chasing the pussy, only to have it get away at the last minute!"

The guys laughed harder and the chief leaned on the counter beside Mark, one hand on the coffee mug Chris had set before him. "It was a couple, three years ago, wasn't it, Adams?"

Chris grunted at him as she began to crack the eggs into a bowl.

"Well, we got this call out to a structure fire, this town house out on the east side. Are you familiar with that area, Will?"

Will shook his head.

"Well, it's a nice neighborhood, but it's not one we go

to much, so we didn't know much about it either. The community there is really friendly, everyone in the area comes out to help."

Mark snickered, the chief looked at him before continuing.

"Adams here wasn't feeling really good that day, and the call caught her in the middle of a nap. I guess she threw her gear on over just a T-shirt and pair of shorts. Anyway, the town house was a great big place and we were there for quite a while. Chris was on Attack that day, and she'd been in a couple times already. She was over in our safe zone, cooling off before going back in. Well, like I said, the neighborhood was really helpful, especially the women. And there are a *lot* of women in that neighborhood. A bunch of them came out with big pitchers of ice water and Gatorade, plastic cups, you know, helping the guys cool off. This was maybe June, July, I don't know, it was hot. And there was Chris, her bunker coat and helmet off, sitting on the curb with her back to the action. I think she was making a little action of her own."

"Yeah, I'll say," Mark interrupted. "That chick was into me, man, into me." He slapped the counter and leaned toward Will. "Oh, she was so hot, you wouldn't even believe it. And I'm telling you, she was making eyes, chatting me up. She was going to give me her phone number, I know she was. Till *she* stepped in." He jerked a thumb at Chris.

Chris rolled her eyes. "She was not *into* you. She was *into* firefighters, and you happened to be there. And she wasn't *some chick* either. Her name was Grace, and she was a very nice lady."

Mark looked at her. "You didn't!"

Chris shrugged and began beating her eggs. The chief looked at them both and back to Will.

"Anyway, Adams was sitting with her back to the fire, and the wind shifted, throwing embers in that direction. One of them went down the back of her bunker pants." The chief joined the guys in their laughter. "So she stands up and drops her pants right there in front of everyone!" He was pounding the counter in his mirth. "She's wearing these sweat shorts, and now there's this big hole burnt in them, her ass hanging out!" He held his hand out as Will began to hold his own belly in laughter. "So then, all these ladies decided to help. They threw everything they had on her! Gatorade, ice water, everything they could get their hands on. They doused her. So her T-shirt is soaked, and her shorts are burnt, nearly gone!"

The chief doubled over laughing. "Those women went nuts! They practically mauled her right there! Oh, man, it took us forever to get rid of them. They started coming by the station, trying to see her. We must have responded to fourteen false alarms in that part of town over the next month, every one of them hoping she'd show up. They all wanted a hunk of that burnin' love!" He wiped his eyes and grinned. "Even that little fox Mark was after! She started calling the station *every day*."

Mark stood up straight, his face immediately sobering. "Hey, you guys never told me she was calling!"

Chris leaned toward him, one elbow on the counter, hand dangling limply from her wrist in a teasing display. "Because she wasn't calling for you, Pepe, she was calling for me."

His eyes widened as he looked at her. "Oh, no! You didn't!"

She grinned devilishly. "You wouldn't have liked her anyway, Mark. She had one hell of a gag reflex."

Mark's mouth fell open. "But . . . but . . . b—"

Before Mark could stop stuttering and get the words formed, the overhead tones went off and Dispatch called them to respond to a car wreck on the interstate. Chris shut off the stove and dropped her pan of eggs into the sink. She clapped Mark on the back as they all ran for their trucks.

Shelby flipped the siren over to phaser mode and yelled at Bryce, "Clear right!"

Bryce nodded and proceeded through the intersection, not even glancing to double check her, having no doubt she was right. He turned the stereo up. Bad Company's "Feel Like Makin' Love" rocked out of his favorite radio station as Shelby turned the siren back to wail. She glanced at her partner and smiled as they both sang along. Bryce always cranked the music when he was headed to something serious; she liked that. And by the sound of it, this car wreck was very serious. She watched for traffic on her side, relaxed and sure of herself. But a small part of her mind was working overtime, going over all her worst accidents, thinking about all possible injuries, hoping there were no children involved in this one.

As they rolled up to the accident, Bryce turned down the music and Shelby killed the siren and told Dispatch they were on scene.

Cars were strewn everywhere, some still on the road, some pulled onto the shoulders. The mid-morning sun shone down, glinting off chrome and shards of glass sprinkled across the highway. Shelby could see three vehicles with obvious damage, but there were at least ten more scattered around the road. They pulled up behind another ambulance and jumped out. Shelby could see three people on backboards. There were two more people in one of the cars, obviously trapped. First responders and firefighters were everywhere, each doing what they were supposed to do. Tori, Ryan and two other officers were directing traffic and controlling the growing crowd. Shelby went to the paramedic from the other ambulance.

"Hey, John, what do you have for me?"

"A problem."

Shelby leaned over his patient, an elderly man strapped to a board. "Tell me about it."

John glanced down, indicating his patient. "Mr. Jones here is a class two, and his wife is a class three." He pointed at a woman strapped to another board just a few steps away from the man they were leaning over, a first responder taking her vital signs. "They were both restrained in this car." He pointed to a big four door car with front end damage. "There's no intrusive damage, but his air bag didn't deploy and he hit the steering wheel, bruising to the chest and abdomen. I'm first on scene, but he is adamant that I transport him and his wife. He's threatening to refuse care."

"Name?"

"Jones."

Shelby leaned over the man and explained that John was the first paramedic on scene and legally could not leave until the last person was ready for transport. Mr. Jones was insistent that only John could take him. She shook her head and looked at John.

"You got another crew coming?"

John tipped his head toward a third ambulance just rolling up on scene. "And a bird on the way."

"Okay. Give me a rundown on everything."

John pointed as he talked. "That one over there is ready to go, the trapped driver's a red, passenger's a yellow for mechanism. The bird's coming in for the driver, both need extrication. And we have the Joneses here, ready to go. I'm calling him a yellow, borderline red, I want him out as soon as possible."

"All these other cars?"

John shook his head. "Not involved, checked them all."

Shelby made the decision almost without thought. "Okay, send that one with that crew, tell me everything you know about the trapped, and take these two out."

John looked relieved. "You'll take command?"

She nodded. "I'll take care of it. Now talk to me."

John yanked off the Incident Commander vest and handed it to Shelby. She slipped it on and helped him load his patients as he told her everything he knew about the scene and patients. Shelby called Dispatch on the portable radio and told them she was taking over as Commander while she made her way to the trapped victims. She leaned in the car and checked on the driver. He was unconscious and his breathing was shallow. Bryce was on the other side of the car checking on the passenger. Someone tapped her on the back. She straightened and turned around.

Chris stood in front of her in full turnout gear, holding the Jaws of Life. She grinned.

"Which side first, Boss?"

Shelby got a thumbs-up from Bryce and pointed to the driver. "This one." Her face was sober. "Make it quick, Chris."

Chris nodded and hefted the Jaws into place next to the doorpost. Shelby stepped back, glanced around to make sure the third ambulance was getting their patients loaded up all right, then settled in to watch her friend work.

Chris handled her equipment nimbly, maneuvering the big hydraulic jaws with apparent ease, although Shelby knew that the Jaws were heavy and bulky. She made it look so easy, as if anyone could do it. But Shelby knew how cumbersome those hydraulic Jaws were, how easily they slid out of place when you were trying to hold them steady. Shelby could see a trickle of sweat running down Chris's cheek and the rigid position of her legs bearing the extra weight of the Jaws and her turnout gear, and she knew how tough a job it really was.

The door latch gave with a pop and Chris handed the Jaws to another firefighter. Shelby stepped up and grabbed the door with her, and they pulled together. There were several pops and a high-pitched squealing sound as the metal scraped against itself and bent back. Shelby felt the wind from the helicopter blowing her hair around her face as the door came open.

Before she could call for them, the first responders were there with the extrication equipment. They untangled the man from the car and put him on a backboard. The flight nurse appeared behind Shelby, and she gave her an oral report as they ran him to the aircraft and loaded him in.

By the time Shelby got back to the car, the firefighters and first responders had already helped Bryce get the passenger out and packaged for transport. She was a seventeen-year-old girl with moderate injuries, but she was hysterical. Shelby tried to calm her as they loaded her into the ambulance, but couldn't. She yelled at the group of firefighters standing at the back of her unit, "I'll need someone in here with me."

Chris yanked off her helmet and turnout coat, revealing a snug blue T-shirt with a Maltese cross embossed on the left breast pocket. Her hair was covered tightly with a bandanna, and her bunker pants were held up by a pair of red suspenders, accentuating her breasts and waistline. She tossed her coat and helmet to one of her crew and jumped in the back of the ambulance. Shelby caught a glimpse of Ryan waving them through as the back doors were closed and Bryce headed the unit toward the hospital.

* * *

Shelby wheeled her patient into the hospital and turned her over to the emergency room staff before she realized that Chris had assisted her all the way in, giving her everything she had needed. They had worked together like a well-oiled machine, and neither of them had said a word.

She clapped Chris on the back as she climbed in the ambulance and they headed for the fire station.

"It sure is good to work with you again, old friend."

Chris grinned. "Yeah, it's been a while, but we've still got it."

"Yes, we do. Hey, you disappeared the other night at the bar. Did you find a little honey in need of your services?"

Chris gazed out the window. Bryce was turning onto the street next to her station. "I guess you could say that."

Shelby looked back through the opening between the back and front of the ambulance. *Something's not right. What's up with her?* "Hey, are you all right?"

Chris shook her head. "Yeah, just a lot on my mind, you know."

"Really, like what?"

She shrugged. "You know, stuff." She tried to change the subject. "Hey, who's the dispatcher on today? I don't know her voice. She sounds good."

Shelby reached back and swatted at her. "You leave her alone! She's a nice girl, and a good dispatcher. She doesn't need you fucking up her life."

Chris opened her eyes wide in mock surprise. "Now, Shelby, you know I'd never do anything to mess up anyone's life!"

"Oh, bullshit, Chris. We lost the last dispatcher you

went out with. You broke her heart and she left us. You just keep your mitts off this one!"

"Yeah, yeah." Chris's grin faded as Bryce pulled over at the station and she climbed out. Shelby rolled down the window.

"We're getting together Saturday in the park, you coming?"

"I don't think so. I think I have a date."

Bryce leaned over toward her and drawled, "It'll be an early day; me and the boys have a gig that night."

"Still drumming with that band, are you, Bryce?"

"Yep! We'll make it big someday, and you can say you knew me when."

Chris grinned back at him. "Yeah, yeah." She looked back at Shelby. "I think I have to pass this one, okay?"

"Okay, sure. I'll see you."

Chris slapped the door and Bryce pulled back into traffic. He glanced at his partner. "Is she okay?"

Shelby shook her head. "I don't know. She seems kind of preoccupied, doesn't she?"

He nodded. "It's probably a woman."

Shelby grinned. "Huh! Knowing Chris, it's probably several women!"

"Lucky dog!"

Tori and Ryan were standing in line at a fast food restaurant when the radio on Ryan's hip called out to them. "Respond to a robbery in progress at Diamond's Jewelry on Market Street. Two suspects, armed and dangerous."

They stepped out of line and ran for the door. Tori jumped behind the wheel while Ryan called en route and snapped the mike back in its holder. He turned to her.

"First that car wreck, now this. We're never going to eat today, are we?"

Tori laughed as she sped around a corner. "It doesn't look like it. Check your gun, Rookie, this might be a rough one."

"Gut feeling?"

She nodded.

"Are your feelings always right?"

"Often enough to trust them. You'll learn it soon enough. We're here."

Ryan radioed in as Tori carefully pulled up on scene. They could see one gunman inside the store. He had his back to the windows and seemed to be yelling at someone on the floor. He glanced over at the register and yelled again.

Ryan and Tori cautiously moved to the door, one on each side, weapons in hand. They looked at each other. Tori pushed open the door and Ryan whirled around the door frame into the store, aiming his gun at the armed man.

"Police. Drop your weapon and turn around slowly, hands up!"

The man turned around and aimed at Ryan. He looked about seventeen and scared to death. Tori aimed at the other man standing by the cash register, and he held his hands up. He was unarmed, and looked even younger. Ryan spoke to the first man.

"Okay, son, drop the gun."

"No! No, I'll shoot! Just back off and let me go!"

Ryan stepped closer. "Son, just calm down. Look around you; what are you going to do? There's no place to run."

The man glanced out the window. There were four more police cars and officers lined up with their guns aimed at him.

"See," Ryan continued, "there's no way out. Just put the gun down, it'll be a hell of a lot easier for you."

Tori slowly made her way around to the side of the

man. She kept one eye on him, one on the other man, as she inched slowly around. She could feel her heart pounding, feel her own pulse all the way to the tips of her fingers. Her mind focused completely on the situation at hand. Everything slowed down, became exceptionally clear. She could hear the faint whimper of one of the people on the floor behind her, Ryan's voice, calm and sane, even her own heartbeat, loud and thumping in her ears. She could see the man's panic building as he shifted his gun back and forth between her and Ryan. She kept moving, making her way to the unarmed man, cuffing him and putting him on the floor without any fuss, hardly even an effort in her heightened state of awareness. She began inching closer to the man with the gun, coming up behind him. Ryan kept talking.

"Come on, man, you don't really want to shoot a cop, do you? You think those guys out there will let you live if you do? I'm one of them, they'll never let you even get to the door. You're young, son, you got a lot ahead of you. Drop the gun now and we'll see what we can do. What do you say?"

He looked confused. He kept shaking his head. He started to lower his gun, and then brought it back up again. Tori could hear his breathing. She could see, and even *feel* his panic.

He's going to snap.

She wanted to shout out to Ryan, to warn him. She knew she couldn't; it might startle the man. She quietly holstered her gun and drew her baton.

"No way, man. I ain't goin' to no prison!" The man's voice was shaky, the panic rising within him easily heard. Tori reached out, her arms feeling like lead, and brought her baton down on the man's gun arm, just as he fired a shot.

"Ryan!" Tori could do no more than call his name as

she brought her baton down on the man's arm, dropping it and tackling him as soon as she felt her blow connect. She knocked him to the ground and followed him down, scrambling to get one knee on his neck, one in the small of his back, and one wrist in a hold as his gun skittered across the floor.

Ryan saw Tori recoil, readying herself, heard her call his name and lunged to his right, vaguely hearing someone scream as glass shattered on his left. Ryan hit the floor and rolled, coming back to his feet with the gun.

"Ryan?" Tori called out to her partner as she handcuffed the man and began pulling him to his feet.

"I'm good, Tori." He looked down at himself as if to make sure. "Good."

Tori smiled as Ryan glanced at the people lying on the floor.

"Anybody hurt?"

No one seemed to be.

"Okay, there should be an ambulance outside to make sure. Then we'll need to take statements from all of you. We appreciate your cooperation, folks."

A few officers came in to take out the prisoners. Ryan's voice had stayed calm throughout the whole incident, though Tori knew he was shaking inside. Her pride in him grew as she clapped him on the back.

"You did a hell of a good job, Partner. I believe I owe you lunch."

"Sounds great, if we ever get the paperwork done."

"That's why God made takeout, honey. These guys can take statements, and we can eat at the station while we write."

Ryan faked a look of orgasmic pleasure. "Takeout! You'll really feed me takeout?"

"Yep!"

His eyes glinted mischievously. "Thank God, a woman who knows how to please me! Will you marry me?"

Tori glanced at the other officers, who were trying to look as if they weren't listening intently. She played along with Ryan's game. "Marry you? Oh, I thought you'd never ask! Let's go make the plans! Let's see, we'll need to look at gowns, interview caterers, and oh! I have to call my mother . . ."

The other officers exchanged confused looks and glanced sideways at Tori and Ryan as the two of them climbed back in their car, laughing.

Chris moved slowly through the thick smoke, unable to see more than two or three feet in front of her. She made her way through the opening of the foyer, not three feet from the front door of the house, and suddenly stopped.

The room, already filled with smoke, became impenetrable. The smoke was a heavy black curtain, almost palpable in its thickness. Chris couldn't see any flames, only thick, black smoke. The air was too hot, too heavy. Even with her air tank she found it difficult to breathe. She felt the hair on the back of her neck prickle through her Nomex hood as her instincts took over.

Dark down. She's going to flash.

Chris saw a flame curling through the air like a wisp of smoke out of the corner of her eye and just had time to think, *snakes, flash is imminent,* as she turned and yelled into her self-contained breathing apparatus, "Get out, get out, *get out!*"

She took two steps and ran into Will, wide-eyed and staring at her through his mask. She pushed his shoulder, spinning him around, grabbed the bottom of his air pack, and began to run, pushing him in front of her. They ran through the foyer door and burst out the front door, Chris automatically rolling to the right, yanking Will off his feet. The fire rolled out the door on their heels. Chris heard it roar and felt the heat through her gear, burning the back of her neck where the hair had been prickling moments before.

Will rolled over and jumped to his feet, yanking his mask off and staring at her.

"What the fuck was that?"

Chris pulled off her own gear, moving farther from the burning house. "Flashover. Didn't you see it?" She peeled off her helmet and hood, grabbing the back of her neck. "Shit!"

Will followed her. "What, what's wrong?"

Chris walked straight to the ambulance standing by, stripping off gear on the way and leaving it where it dropped. Will followed her, picking up her dropped gear as he went. She stepped up to the crew.

"Hey, guys, you mind taking a look at this for me?"

She turned around, showing them the back of her neck, hands, and wrists. They examined her closely.

"Looks like a first degree, borderline second. You want us to bandage it for you?"

She shook her head. "No, not if there's no broken skin. Thanks, guys."

Will followed Chris as she made her way back to the truck. "You okay, Chris? Did it get you? What happened?"

She reached the truck and spun around, beginning to take her gear from him. "You didn't see it?"

"No. It was so dark, I couldn't see a thing."

"Did you feel it?"

"Yeah, heavy, black. I thought I saw flames . . ."

"What do you know about flashover?"

He tilted his head. "I know that everything in the area reaches ignition temperature at the same time, even the smoke starts to burn. When it all ignites, you have a heat inversion for about two-and-a-half seconds, and you'll die if you're caught in it. Temperatures of twenty-five hundred and up."

She smiled. "Yes, but do you know what it looks like, what it *feels* like?"

"Um . . ."

"Now you do."

He stopped and stared at her, suddenly realizing what they had just been through. Chris reached out and put a hand on his shoulder, her voice calm and gentle. "Just do me one favor, will you?"

He shrugged. "Anything."

"When I tell you to get out, get the fuck out. Okay?"

He nodded, wide-eyed as she took the rest of her gear out of his arms.

Chapter Six

Laura stood in the bookstore, shelving the new shipment. She had burned French Vanilla incense that morning, thinking of Chris and wishing she had the courage to call her. She placed the books on the shelf slowly, lost in her thoughts of Chris and why she hadn't called. She placed the last book from the box on the shelf and slid her hand down its binding as she turned around, and jumped.

Chris stood there, watching her. She had her arms crossed, leaning her weight on one shoulder casually placed into a corner, and one long jean-clad leg crossed over the other. She wore a bemused smile that suddenly infuriated Laura.

"God, do you always sneak up on people?"

Chris pushed herself out of the corner, dropping her hands to her pockets. "Only if I like them. I never did get that dance you promised me. Are you busy today?"

"I wouldn't have been if you would have called and asked me not to be." As soon as the words left her mouth, Laura regretted them. *I just sounded like a total bitch. Why did I do that?*

Chris raised an eyebrow. "I would have called, but you didn't give me your number. I gave you mine, remember?

And *you* didn't call *me*. I had to track you down here, because I don't even know your last name."

Laura was suddenly embarrassed for being angry with her. *Of course she couldn't call me, and I didn't have the guts to call her. Stupid, Laura, stupid.* "I'm sorry, I was going to call, I just . . ."

Chris smiled. "It's okay, really. But I would like to know your last name."

Laura blushed. "Deerhardt."

"Dearheart?"

"Yes, but not spelled that way."

Chris closed her eyes and savored the name on her lips, whispering it to herself before opening her eyes and piercing Laura's soul. "So how busy are you?"

"I've got a couple hours worth of shelving and storing. After that, I guess I could skip out, providing Hannah doesn't have any plans."

"Let me help you."

Laura was startled. "You want to help me? Why would you want to do that?"

Chris looked at her and smiled, turning on her charm. "Why? To help you. To spend a little time with you. I'd enjoy it." *And I could so easily enjoy you, Laura Dear Heart.*

"You'd be bored!"

Chris stepped up and took a book from her, brushing her hand with her own as if by accident. "No, I don't think I will."

Laura almost shivered when their hands touched. *Does she have any idea what she does to me? She must, I can't be hiding it that well.* "Well, I guess I could use some help. But if you get bored, just tell me. I can spend all day with books."

Chris grinned devilishly. "Oh, I'll let you know if I'm bored, all right."

Chris handed Laura new books to put on the shelf and took old ones from her, boxing them as they went. They chatted easily about some of their favorites while they worked. Chris watched the younger woman, fascinated with her every move. Laura didn't seem to notice the way she handled the books. She didn't just put them on the shelf, she touched them lovingly, as if she was caressing the faces of old friends. Her hands made Chris think of two perfectly matched ballerinas: fluid, graceful, moving in harmony, dancing not only to the music of life, but with each other, complementing each other's every move. They were tiny compared to her own, yet supple and strong, the fingers straight and slim, each tipped with a conservative, well-manicured nail.

Chris could just imagine those hands touching her skin, caressing, sending chills down her spine. She closed her eyes and shivered a little, imagining, anticipating . . .

"Chris?"

"What?" She realized that Laura had been talking and she hadn't heard a word.

"Are you here?"

"Yeah, yeah, I'm sorry. I was just . . ." Laura was looking at her expectantly. "Your hands are . . . beautiful." Chris reached over and touched one lightly with one finger.

"Thanks." Laura flushed a bright red. *One finger on my hand . . . I never imagined a touch could be so . . . compelling.* She moved her hand back out of Chris's reach. "Want to help me take these boxes back to storage?"

She nodded and picked up a box, following Laura to a room in the back of the store, watching her move beneath her tan slacks. They entered a dimly lit room crowded with boxes stacked in neat rows, up to six feet high in some places. Laura led her down one of the rows and they deposited their burdens. Laura turned around and stepped directly into her arms.

They were both stunned a moment, then Chris circled her arms around Laura and kissed her softly. Laura began to respond to the kiss, and then pushed away.

Chris stepped back and held her hands up, as if to show she had no weapons. "I'm sorry, Laura. I guess I just overstepped your boundaries. I'm sorry."

She turned to leave. Laura caught her arm.

"No, don't go." She sighed. "You didn't overstep anything. I . . . I wanted you to kiss me. I just, I don't know. I . . ."

Chris studied her face as her words trailed off to a shake of her head. "You've never kissed a woman before, have you, Laura?"

Laura dropped her head. "No."

Chris took Laura's hands in hers, her mind still marveling at them. *They're so soft; how can anything be this soft and this strong?* "It's all right. I'm not going to ask you to do anything you don't want to. I like you very much, but if you don't want more than friendship, that's okay."

Laura looked up into her eyes, those blue eyes that felt like they pierced her soul. "But I do want more. I've always wanted . . ." *What? You've always wanted what? A woman? No, I don't think so. A friend? Maybe. Maybe just that . . . spark. And God knows she sparks.* "I don't know." She paused, gathering her thoughts, trying to get them in some order. "I have feelings for you. And that's new for me. I've never felt attraction for a woman before. Hell, I'm not sure I've ever felt like *this* for anyone before. I just don't know what to do about it." She looked down at the floor. "I'm sure you think that's pretty silly."

Chris lifted Laura's chin and smiled into her soft brown eyes. *I could drown in those eyes. Can she tell? Do I want her to know?* "I don't think it's silly. Not at all. I understand anything new or different than what you expect can be a little scary."

Laura looked up at Chris. "I'm not exactly scared, just . . ." she trailed off, her lips slightly parted, her eyes locked into Chris's gaze.

"Scared, confused, whatever you're feeling, it's okay." Chris caught herself leaning toward her, as if for a kiss, and broke herself away. She gave her a disarming smile, her voice becoming light. "Why don't we finish stocking? Then we'll get out of here."

Laura took a deep breath, relief washing over her mind. "Okay."

Chris's smile faded as Laura turned away. *I could do that. I could ease her mind and teach her this dance. And how I want to.* She watched Laura from behind as she followed her back out of the storeroom. *So what's stopping me?*

The afternoon sun was bright, but there was a cool breeze blowing through the park. Tori and Shelby were setting up a picnic lunch with Bryce and his wife, Susan, while the kids played. Tori saw a small expensive-looking convertible pull up and knew it had to be David.

"Hey, guys, Ryan brought a friend."

David and Ryan joined them, and Tori introduced everyone. David greeted everyone with his usual formality before singling out Susan and sticking with her. Ryan sat next to Tori and watched the kids rolling in the grass, playing a late-summer game that only children could understand.

River, the youngest, seemed fascinated with Ryan. Before long, she left the game and curled up on the bench beside him, laying her head in his lap and napping. He watched her sleep until Bryce and Shelby started tossing a football around. River got up and joined the makeshift football game. Ryan watched her play, and then looked at Tori gathering up the trash from their picnic.

"She's yours." It was more a statement than a question. River looked so much like Tori that it would have been hard not to notice.

"Yes. River and the boy, Casey, are both mine."

"Do you mind if I ask how?"

Tori laughed an easy, comfortable laugh. "The usual way. I was married."

"Really? What happened?"

"Honestly?"

He shrugged. "I'm just curious."

She looked at her partner for a moment before sitting down beside him. "We were married young. You know, there were a lot of things we didn't know, and a lot of things he couldn't handle."

Ryan raised his eyebrows. "Like? Or am I getting too personal?"

"You're my partner, nothing's too personal." She sighed. "He was a lawyer, and thought when his career got going I should stay home and raise the kids. He thought me being a cop was just a phase. He didn't want me to work at all. And I figured out that I didn't want him at all."

Ryan laughed. "How'd you figure that one out?"

Tori laughed with him. "Actually, he helped. I hadn't ever thought about it. I mean, you're raised believing that you're going to find a good man, settle down, have kids, live happily ever after. Your momma never mentions that your 'good man' might want to swing a little to spice up your life."

Ryan's eyes widened in disbelief. "Swing? No way!"

Tori laughed again. "Oh, yes! He wanted to play with other women. I agreed to it, never suspecting that I'd like it. The more we did it, the less I wanted him around."

She grinned. "It really is funny when you think about it. He thought that involving other women would make it more fun for him, but it just made me want him less!"

Ryan was laughing, that silent laugh that had amazed Tori before. She laughed with him and took a deep breath. "He got pretty upset when I didn't want him anymore, so he found himself a girlfriend. Since he had one, I figured it was only fair that I could have one, too. How was I to know it was the same chick?"

Ryan wiped tears from his eyes. "You're kidding me!"

"That's what he said when he came home early and found us! You should have seen the look on his face!"

"Oh, my God, stop! I can't take any more, you're killing me!" He held his stomach as he wiped away his tears again.

Tori nodded, faking a grave expression. "He said that, too!"

Tori and Ryan watched the kids play until he could look at her again without laughing. He watched as Shelby hit the ground, a pile of children on top of her. "Was Shelby married, too?"

"No. Shelby always knew what she wanted. She just wanted a kid, not a man. So she went the old artificial route. Luck of the draw, she ended up with twins, Sammy and Erica. They were two when I met them, River was just an infant. Casey was three, and he's the only one who remembers when we weren't all a family."

"So it's never been a problem, raising kids in a gay family?"

Tori shook her head and swept her loose hair behind her shoulder. "No more than any other family, I think. Sometimes River gives Shelby some grief. You know, the old 'you're not my mother routine,' but no more than any other child does with a stepparent. We've always considered the kids *ours*, not hers and mine."

"Do they ever see their fathers?"

"No. The twins know they don't have one, and my ex chooses not to have contact. My brother, Steve, watches them when we work our night rotations, and we have plenty of friends, so they have men around." She shrugged. "We do okay."

Ryan had a dreamy look on his face, and it was Tori's turn to raise her eyebrows.

"You want kids?"

"Oh, someday, maybe." He shrugged and said it casually, but the dreamy look didn't leave his face. "It's just, you know, work and the closet and everything. I'm not ready to come out to those guys. I'm just not."

Tori nodded. "I don't blame you there."

"You're really brave, you know. To be so out at work. I sometimes wish I could do that."

"It's your choice, Partner. They treat men differently in this job, and it probably would be harder for you. I may not have come out, but I couldn't really hide Shelby."

Shelby ran by, football in hand, and Casey tackled her. She rolled over and sat up. "Hey, you guys want to help us out here? The kids are kicking our butts!"

Tori laughed. "Serves you right! Where's Chris? I thought she was coming."

Shelby shrugged and got to her feet. "She said something about a date. Come on, we need you out here."

David and Susan declined. Ryan clapped Tori on the back and they got up to join the game.

Chris pulled her motorcycle up behind Laura's car and shut the engine off. Laura got off the bike with a little hop and pulled the helmet off her head. She handed it to Chris and ran a hand through her hair, tousling it.

"Thanks for showing me around."

Chris smiled. "I enjoyed it."

Laura ducked her head a little and smiled back. "Me, too. Hey, why don't you come over to my place for a while? Maybe we could talk."

Chris looked at her. *She's so incredible. Do I really want to do this?* "I think I'd like that. I'll follow you."

Laura unlocked the door to her apartment and opened it. "Make yourself at home, I'm going to get comfortable." She headed toward what Chris assumed was the bedroom.

Chris stepped through the door of the apartment and instantly felt something she had never felt before. She had been in countless apartments and houses, but had never felt so at home anywhere other than her own place.

It was a small apartment, without a lot of furniture, but it was immaculately clean. There were a lot of trinkets, mostly fantasy figurines. Laura had placed candles on almost every shelf and table. An entertainment center took up most of the wall opposite the sofa, and a very old oak desk dominated one corner. Chris could smell vanilla and noticed the incense burner on the desk. She smiled.

She's hooked. Am I sure I want that?

She walked around the front room, liking the simple way Laura decorated. She stopped in front of a bookshelf by the desk. It was full of books, from classic titles that looked like antiques to recent best-sellers. She reached out and touched one, a huge volume bound in leather with gilded lettering, thinking of the way Laura had caressed the books at the store earlier that day.

Does she touch this one the same? Would she touch me that way?

Laura yelled from the bedroom, "Hey, you like wine?"

Chris closed her eyes as she ran her fingers across the lettering. "Sure."

"There are a couple bottles in the fridge, and you'll

find glasses to the left of the sink. Why don't you pour us some?"

Chris went to the kitchen and found the wine and glasses. She was pouring when Laura came in. She handed her a glass. "I like your apartment. It feels," she paused, looking for the right words, "comfortable. Homey, as if you've been here a long time."

"Thanks." She shrugged. "I really didn't have anything except my desk when I moved in, and some of the small things I've been collecting over the years." She tossed her hand, as if it didn't matter. "It's starting to feel like home. Let's go sit down."

Chris followed her into the living room. Laura turned on the stereo. "What kind of music do you like?"

Chris stopped and sat on the floor in front of the stereo. "I like everything." She started looking through Laura's CDs, all neatly placed alphabetically in racks. "You're a country fan."

"Some. There's rock and pop in the other rack."

Chris looked through them. "You like the blues?"

"Sure, what I've heard. I don't have any, though."

Chris put up a finger in a wait gesture, and drained her glass. "I do. Hang on, I'll get it."

"You carry CDs on your motorcycle?"

"Doesn't everyone? Built-in stereo, storage under the seat, it's got the works. I'll be right back."

Laura shook her head in amazement and went to the kitchen to pour more wine. She liked this woman, and wanted to know everything about her. She was more surprised and amazed with every answer she got.

Chris came back in holding four CDs. "I don't carry much with me, but I brought up what I have." She took the full wineglass Laura offered her. "What would you like to hear?"

Laura curled her legs under herself on the sofa. "They're yours, you pick."

Chris loaded the player and sat down next to her. "This is one of my favorites. It's got a really prominent bass, kind of . . . slinky."

"Slinky?" Laura laughed.

"Yeah, slinky. Very sexy."

They talked and listened to the music. Before either of them knew it, the wine bottle was empty. Laura opened the second bottle and put on another CD.

Chris cocked her head to one side and listened. "What's this?"

"One of *my* favorites. Sarah McLachlan, *Fumbling Towards Ecstasy*. Not slinky, but very erotic."

Chris leaned her head back and closed her eyes, listening, letting the music flow around her. *She's right. Not sexy, erotic.*

Laura watched her, sitting so easily, so comfortable with herself, and felt a pull. *My God, she's so beautiful. I'm not sure I could resist her if I tried. But why try? Why not just . . .* She leaned over and kissed her.

Chris kissed back, exploring Laura's mouth with her tongue, tasting the wine on her lips. She opened her eyes. Laura was looking at her. She recognized the look, she'd seen it enough before. It was longing. Chris touched her face, lightly running her fingers over the bone structure, feeling the softness of her skin. Laura returned the touch, and it was everything Chris had imagined it would be. Suddenly, she felt hot as Laura whispered softly, "Teach me, Chris. Teach me to love a woman."

Chris smiled, her face serene despite the battle raging inside her body to keep her desire in check. "I can't teach you love, Laura."

"You know what I mean."

"Yes, I do. And I want to, more than you know. But I'm not sure you really want that."

"What if I do?" Laura leaned in for another kiss.

Chris caught her face and looked into her eyes. *What if she does? God, why do I want her so badly?* "Right now, just let me hold you."

Laura laid her head on Chris's shoulder, and Chris held her.

Chris opened her eyes at the sound of her pager alarm, realizing she had fallen asleep on the sofa, Laura in her arms. She could feel the residue of wine in her head and mouth, and a twinge in her shoulder as she lifted her arm slowly, trying not to wake Laura.

God, I'm getting old.

Laura groaned and rolled over when Chris slid out from beneath her. She wrote her pager number on a slip of paper and laid it on the coffee table. She leaned over and gently kissed Laura's cheek before slipping out the door.

Chapter Seven

Bryce came running out the door of the ambulance base when Shelby pulled up for work. She jumped out of her car. "What, we've got a call already?"

Bryce was laughing. "No, no." He gave her a big hug, sweeping her off her feet and twirling her around before setting her back down. "It's bigger than that! The whole board is inside, and the CISD team, too."

"What the hell is going on?"

He hugged her again. "Mike's been canned! He's in there packing his shit right now! I think they're going to offer the position to you."

Shelby stopped short and stared at him. "No way! I put in for that six months ago; why in the world would they offer it to me now?"

"Because Mike's been fired. Hello, have you been listening? Nobody else here wants it, you'll be perfect."

"Okay, I'm lost."

"Come over here and sit down, I'll tell you everything."

Bryce took Shelby's briefcase from her hand and put his arm around her, making her feel like a little girl tucked against his large frame. He steered her over to the garage and sat her down on a bench.

"Okay, here's the scoop. You and Mike both put in for the supervisor's position six months ago, right?"

She shrugged. "Sure, but he got it."

"Yeah, but he's been screwing up ever since. We knew he would, 'cause he's an idiot, but we didn't know that the board's been tracking him. He's been written up on . . . hang on," he pulled a folded piece of paper out of his pocket and looked at it. "Seven major rule violations in the past three months."

"What?"

"Yeah! They wouldn't tell us what all of them were, but the last straw was yesterday. It seems our fearless leader," he read from the paper, "contributed to the death of a patient through gross negligence."

Shelby's eyes widened. "No! Mike killed someone? Come on, he's an asshole, but he's not a murderer! Besides, yesterday was Sunday, he never works weekends. He couldn't have done it."

"He wasn't working. I guess he was hanging out at home with the scanner on. He heard a call in his neighborhood and decided to first respond. When he got there, he realized the patient was a frequent flier. You know that old guy with the chest pain that always turns out to be nothing? Over on Seventh?"

Shelby rolled her eyes up as if she was scanning her memory visually. "Angina and heartburn, the guy's name is Compbell, or Compburn, something like that. He must call a couple times a month, sometimes more."

"Yeah, that guy. Mike realized it was him and told the crew to reduce code. Then he gave the guy two nitro."

Shelby nodded. "He always takes nitro."

Bryce shook his head. "He always takes it *before he calls*. He'd already taken *four*. Mike gave him two more."

"And bottomed out his blood pressure." She closed her eyes. "Mike didn't even ask if he had taken any?"

Bryce shook his head. "Nope. No history, nothing. Mike just figured it was nothing. He even had a cuff and didn't bother to take vitals. It was the real thing this time, he was having the big one. The guy dropped before the crew could get there."

"Full arrest?"

"Yep."

"Oh, that poor family."

He nodded gravely. "It gets worse. Mike jumps on the unit, I don't know why, maybe to try and fix it before anyone notices, and rides in to the hospital. Whatever, the guy didn't make it. And, get this, turns out the guy is a personal friend of Dr. Smith."

"The Medical Director? That Dr. Smith?"

"The one and only. And guess who's working ER weekend rotation?"

Shelby's mouth dropped open. "No!"

"Yep! You guessed it! Smith went over that run with a fine-toothed comb. He threw a fit when he found out what happened, and demanded Mike's termination *immediately*."

"There's going to be lawsuits rolling through here. That poor family."

Bryce shook his head, his eyes sparkling. "Nope. The family found out that suing the department would come back on Doc Smith. They're suing for wrongful death against Mike personally."

Her eyebrows raised in surprise. "Him personally? Oh, man, he'll lose his license, maybe spend jail time."

"He should! You know how dangerous he is out there! You remember that woman in the MVA a couple years ago."

She shook her head. "But you know she probably wouldn't have made it anyway."

"No, but his incompetence didn't let us find out for sure, did it?"

Shelby rubbed her face. *Can't argue with that one. His triage skills suck. He never even gave her a chance.* "No, I guess not."

"And countless other calls we could bring up where he fucked up. And that's just what we know about." Bryce punched his fist hard into his open hand, his slow drawl beginning to sound dangerous. "Mike's incompetent. He's a shitty medic, and this just proves it. He doesn't deserve to wear this uniform. Those people called for help, and they got death. I hope they throw the book at him!"

"No shit," Shelby agreed. "The team's here to debrief the crew that hauled him?"

"They did that early this morning. I guess they're talking to us today. They'll be starting here in a few minutes."

Shelby nodded. "Is Chris here for this one?"

"Yep, I saw her inside just before you pulled up. Man, I can't believe this is really happening. The board has called a meeting right after the debriefing. They're going to discuss appointing a new supervisor. It's gonna be you, Shelby, I just know it."

She shrugged. "Maybe. We better go in, they'll be waiting on us."

They started to go in when Cindy, a new EMT, came through the garage door, running into Bryce. She looked nervous as she mumbled an apology, took out a pack of cigarettes, shook one out and lit it. Shelby motioned Bryce in and walked over to the young woman.

"Got a spare?"

Cindy handed her a cigarette. Shelby lit it, took a long drag and looked at it, coughing. "I quit these things a while back. They'll kill you, you know."

Cindy shrugged and mumbled something Shelby couldn't hear. Shelby turned to her.

"Hey, you look a little shaken. What's wrong?"

Cindy took a long drag and blew out smoke. "It's this whole thing. I'm really nervous."

I see that. "Why? What's there to be nervous about?"

"The last thing Mike did was hire me, and now he's fired, and I'm not even trained yet. I don't know what's going to happen to me. All these people are here . . . . I don't think I can talk to them."

Shelby sympathized with the girl, but was a little amused. "How old are you, Cindy?" *No more than a baby, I'm sure.*

"Twenty-two."

Just what I thought, a pup. Oh, we do get them young these days. "How long have you had your license?"

"A month."

"And you've been here what, a week?"

She nodded, blowing more smoke. Shelby smiled, trying not to let out a small laugh.

"Look, just because you were hired by Mike doesn't mean you'll get fired with him. Nobody holds that against you."

"But no one is talking to me. All I know is what I read in that memo, about him being fired and all of us having this big meeting. People get real quiet when I walk in the room. I don't think anyone here likes me."

Shelby laughed. *Was I ever that green? I guess I was, but things were different then.* "Don't be so paranoid. People don't talk to you because they don't know you. We tend to be a really tight group here, and it takes a while before you're fully trusted."

She reached over and put her hand on Cindy's shoulder. "I know, it doesn't seem fair, but you have to prove yourself before you really become part of us. Not just as an EMT, but also as a person. You see, most of us don't even have any friends outside of the emergency services field. And we're more than friends, we're family. We depend on each other, sometimes for our lives. It takes a while to build that kind of trust."

Cindy made a disgusted noise. "I'll never be trusted as an EMT, much less a person."

Shelby shook her head and smiled. *Fantastic, she's young, green, and jaded. This is going to be tough.* "Who have you been running with?"

"Um, the tall guy with the beard. Fred."

So that's what did it. Hell, running with Fred might make me paranoid. She shrugged nonchalantly. "Oh, well, no wonder. Fred's a dinosaur; he's been in EMS since the dawn of time, almost as long as I have. He doesn't like new people." *Or new ideas, or changes, even women in the field . . . God, Shelby, you've got your work cut out for you if you really get this position. What the hell will you do with Fred?*

Cindy looked at her pleadingly, searching for some explanation, some acceptance. "But *you're* not like that."

"That's because I'm not afraid of change." *And I'm not a burnt-out prick.* "Fred's a good medic, but he doesn't like anything new, including people. Why don't I talk to some people and try to get you put with someone else?"

"You could do that?"

"Well, I can't promise anything, but it couldn't hurt to try."

"Could I train with you?"

"I don't know, Bryce has been mine for so long, he and I work so well together that I'm not sure we're the right crew to train . . ." She watched Cindy's hopeful look fall. "But we'll see what we can do, okay?"

Cindy sighed and flipped her cigarette out the bay door. "Thanks, Shelby. I appreciate you helping me out like this."

"No problem. Now, you're worried about the debriefing?"

She nodded. "A little."

"They're here to help us deal with our stress. I've been through this a million times; never once did I regret it. We're just going to sit down and talk. No one blames anyone, and you'll learn a lot about dealing with the stress in this job, and in your real life. You know, the one away from here."

"Do we really need that?"

"Yes, we do. You'd be surprised how much."

She sighed. "Okay."

Chris poked her head out the door. "Hey, Shel, we're waiting on you."

Shelby nodded and headed toward her. "Chris, this is Cindy. It's her first time and she's a little nervous."

"Perfectly natural." Chris gave her a disarming grin. "Come on in, Cindy, I promise it won't hurt."

Laura walked into the bookstore a little after opening time. She looked at Hannah.

"Thanks for opening up this morning, Hannah. I just couldn't get here."

"I'll bet. Up late last night, were you?" Hannah laughed at the incredulous look Laura gave her. "What, did you really think I wouldn't notice? And if I'm worth my salt, I'd say it had something to do with Chris."

Laura pulled a slip of paper out of her pocket and waved it. "Her pager number. I need to call it; she sneaked out this morning without saying good-bye."

Hannah raised her eyebrows in surprise. "She gave you her personal pager number?"

"Yes."

"Wow, that must have been some night."

Laura went behind the counter and stashed her backpack. "Why?"

Hannah leaned over the counter and looked at her.

"Are you kidding? Chris doesn't give out her pager number. She doesn't even give out her home number."

"Really?"

"Really! I know people who would pay you well for that number."

"Why? I mean, why doesn't she give it out?"

Hannah shook her head. "Because, child, if she gave out her number she could be contacted."

"And that would be a bad thing?"

"For Chris? That would be a nightmare. She'd never have any peace."

"She's that popular, huh?"

Hannah laughed. "Popular is an understatement. Chris is more like a goddess. Everyone wants a piece of her. She's the trophy everyone wants on their arm. She's the wild heart that everyone wants to tame. But no one can. Oh, they can have her for a night, but after that she's gone. No note, no contact, and definitely no pager number." Hannah leaned in closer. "So what did you do?"

Laura looked wide-eyed at her. "Nothing. She came over, we talked a lot, drank a little wine. We fell asleep."

"No sex?"

Laura shook her head.

"Why not?"

She shrugged. "I don't know. I guess she knew I wasn't ready. I thought I was. But now I'm glad I didn't. Maybe this isn't for me after all."

"What isn't for you?"

"This. This lifestyle. Maybe I just need to be somewhere else."

"But how do you *feel*?"

Laura ran a hand through her hair. "Fantastic. Disappointed. Scared. I don't know . . . confused. I don't know what I want. I don't know who I am. God, Hannah, what's wrong with me?"

Hannah straightened up and laughed. "Wrong with you? Nothing's wrong with you, child. You just need to know who you are before you can give yourself to anyone else. And I expect that you'll have to convince Chris after you find yourself."

"And how do I do that?"

"Convince Chris? Honey, she's an ox. You treat her like one. You hit her over the head with the facts until she starts to listen."

"No, how do I find myself?"

Hannah looked at Laura seriously, her voice low and soothing. "You go deep within, to your heart. That's the only place you can make sure it's you, and not some other influence upon your mind. Within yourself, you can find the answers to everything you need to know."

"You make it sound so easy."

Hannah smiled. "It becomes easy, after a while." She reached over and slid a chair to herself, settling into it. "Are you ready for your first lesson?"

Laura closed her eyes. "Yes."

Ryan flipped off the siren and carefully pulled the cruiser over and put it in park, leaving his lights flashing. He spoke to Tori without taking his eyes off the car they had pulled over.

"Why do I want to search that car?"

"Your gut's talking to you, Partner. Mine says the same thing. Let's see if we can get probable cause on this guy."

They climbed out of their cruiser and approached the car. It was a new Mercedes, all the windows darkened as much as the law would allow. Ryan approached the driver's door, keeping his body close to the car, casually touching the trunk as he passed.

Good boy. Tori held back her smile as she hung back, stopping right at the doorpost on the passenger side and looking through the dark glass. She couldn't see anyone in the car except the driver, but she noticed a large gym bag tossed on the backseat. Ryan bent slightly to look in at the driver.

"Good afternoon, sir. I need to see your license, registration, and proof of insurance, please."

The man handed over the requested paperwork and Ryan studied it for a moment.

"Mr. Cowlin, do you know why I stopped you today?"

The man rolled his eyes. "You need to fill a quota?"

Ryan let the comment slide by him. "Sir, you were doing forty-seven in a thirty-five zone."

"I don't think I was."

"Yes, sir, I clocked you."

"Then write me a fuckin' ticket. We'll discuss it in court."

Ryan walked back to his car and called the license in to Dispatch. Tori leaned down by the passenger side of the cruiser, not taking her eyes off the man in the other car.

"What's up?"

Ryan sighed. "I'm running a twenty-eight, twenty-nine. I don't like this guy, he's aggressive. Did you see the gym bag?"

"Yes. And something tells me it's not basketball shorts in there. He's aggressive?" A red flag was waving in Tori's mind.

"Not enough for PC, just enough to be an asshole."

The radio squawked, Ryan cursed. "Nothing. Damn it!"

Tori shrugged. "We've still got the speeding. And if he's as dumb as he looks he'll let us search the car."

"I don't think so, but we can give it a try." Ryan wrote the speeding ticket and walked back to the driver. "Mr. Cowlin, I need you to sign on that line by the X." The man reached through the window and took the clipboard from Ryan. He signed his name and held it back out the window.

Tori leaned down by his passenger window. "Sir, what's in the bag in the back?"

The man turned to her, glanced at her name tag, and studied her face. "None of your damn business, Officer Pataki." He spit her name out with a sneer.

Ryan took the clipboard back from the man. "Mr. Cowlin, do you mind if we take a look in your car?"

"What, do you think I'm stupid? You don't have probable cause to search my car. You take yourselves back to your station and get a warrant, and then you can look at my ride. Until then, leave me the fuck alone. Can I go now?"

"Yes, sir." Ryan handed the man back his paperwork and stepped away from the car. The man threw one last sneer at them both and pulled away. Ryan stepped over to Tori.

"Man, I didn't like that. Did he make you nervous? The way he looked at us . . . man!"

Tori nodded. "Yeah, like he was studying us, like he wanted to remember our faces." She shivered. "That guy's dirty, Partner. You mark my words."

Ryan shook his head as he walked back to the car. "You're not kidding. God, I hope we never see him again."

The debriefing lasted over an hour, after which everyone got up for a break. Shelby tried to catch Chris, but Cindy caught her first.

"I just wanted to thank you, Shelby, for talking to me outside."

Shelby looked over Cindy's shoulder, searching the crowded room for Chris. "No problem, Cindy, anytime." She caught sight of Chris slipping out the door. "I'll catch up to you later, okay?"

She brushed by Cindy and headed for the door. As she reached out to open it, the president of the board caught her arm.

"Shelby, we need to meet with you and the other employees."

"Yes, sir, when would you like to do that?"

"Right now."

Shelby gave one last look at the door and nodded. "All right. I guess we're all mostly here."

"You want to gather them up for me?"

"Sure." She turned to face the room of people and raised her voice above the noise level. "Hey, guys, the board's ready to meet with us; you want to gather back at the table please?"

The employees quickly gathered around and sat back down, facing the panel of board members. The president cleared his throat.

"As you all know, Mike is no longer an employee here. His position needs to be filled immediately, and we'd like to ask for your input. We can post this position nationally, or fill it from within. We'd like to fill it from within, if you're agreeable to that. Miss Tucker, you expressed interest several months ago, is that still on your agenda?"

Shelby glanced around the room and was met by smiling faces and a thumbs-up from Bryce. She turned back to the panel in front of her. "Well, yes, I'd be interested in the position, providing the crews here will have me."

The president laughed. "Have you? They've almost insisted. We, the board, will support your nomination, providing you can give an adequate explanation for this." He held up a state trip ticket filled out in her handwriting. "Can you?"

Shelby raised her eyebrows. "I don't know. What is it?"

He slid the paper over to her. "A call you took a few days ago. You took over Incident Command without consulting your superiors. Can you explain why?"

Shelby slid the paper back to him after a cursory glance at it. "I didn't have a superior on scene to consult. There wasn't time to call anyone. I made the decision, and I stand behind it."

"Why was it necessary? John was Commander on scene, he's as highly trained as you; why couldn't he keep his post?"

"John had a patient insisting that only he could transport. He was threatening to refuse care."

"Who transports isn't the patient's decision, refusal is his option."

"That's right. But both John and I felt that he needed care, and that harm would have come to the patient had he not been transported. We did what we had to in order to ensure that he went to the hospital."

"And that was your decision, or you and John made it together?"

"It was my decision."

John spoke up. "Sir, if I may, I stand behind Shelby's decision. That patient ended up having a cardiac contusion."

"Cardiac contusion? I'm a businessman, not a doctor. Speak to me in English."

"His heart was bruised. He could have died without treatment."

"I see. I spoke to Mike after this call, and he didn't agree with the changing of Incident Command. He said it wasn't something he'd have done."

Bryce rolled his eyes. "That's because Mike didn't have the ba—"

"Bryce!" Shelby cut him short with a sharp look and

turned back to the board. "No, Mike wouldn't have made the same decision. And I'm sure you'll find that Mike wouldn't agree with some of the other decisions I'll make if you put me in this position. But I stand behind it. I believe that harm would have come to the patient if we had done anything else. Our first rule is 'do no harm,' and that's what I chose to follow. If that keeps me out of this position, so be it. It was the right decision."

The president leaned over to listen to something the secretary said to him, and then cleared his throat. "Okay, do we need to do a secret ballot on this, or are you all agreeable to Miss Tucker as your supervisor?"

He looked around the room in silence for a moment, waiting for some argument from someone. He only received nods of agreement. "Okay then. We're going to executive; if you all will step out, we'll call you back in when the decision is made."

The employees all stood and shuffled out the door into the bay. Shelby leaned on the nearest ambulance and let out a sigh of relief. Bryce punched her on the shoulder.

"It's yours, Shel, I know it is. God, this is *great!*"

She smiled wearily at him. "Thanks, Bry. Are you guys sure about this?"

She was met with a chorus of positive replies.

"Okay, as long as you guys are sure, I'll do it."

Chris rode her bike back to the fire station. She walked in and tossed her jacket on the back of a chair, looking around the room at her crew watching TV. Her eyes settled on Joe, the guy who had come in to cover for her while she took care of the debriefing. She smiled and called out to him, "Hey, Joe, have you been keeping these guys in line for me?"

"Sure have. It's been so good to be here again! I almost don't want to leave."

"Well, why don't you stay awhile longer? I'd like to get a full workout without interruption for a change."

"Hey, no problem, I'd love to."

Chris checked her pager before she changed into her workout gear and headed to the gym equipment. *Still no call from Laura. What did I do wrong? Why won't she call?*

She swung her leg over the weight bench and lay back, settling her shoulders before lifting the heavy bar. She pressed the bar up and down, counting repetitions, working her body to try to clear her thoughts. *Why do I want her to call? Do I really want her that bad?*

She finished her first set on the bench press and went to the rowing machine. *I've got to get her off my mind. She's no good for me. She's just a girl, she doesn't even know what she wants.* She rowed and the evaporation of sweat began to cool her skin as her thoughts kept time to her movements. *I could show her what she wants. She told me she wanted me to. So why don't I? What's wrong with giving her what she wants?* She pushed her body harder, sweat falling into her eyes, her shirt clinging to her, her breathing hard and fast. *Because she doesn't really know what she wants. And why do I even care?*

"Shit!" Chris stopped rowing and wiped her face with the collar of her shirt. She heard someone in the doorway clear his throat and jumped, looking up.

"Oh, Chief, I didn't see you there."

"No, you didn't. And that's a little weird for you. What's up with you, Chris?"

She shrugged and moved on to the leg press. "Nothing, Chief, I'm good."

He walked over to her and watched her press the weights. "No, you're not. I would never have been able to stand there without you knowing it if you were good. Something's eating you. Is it me? Did I upset you the other day with the new guy?"

Chris smiled and let out her breath hard as she worked her legs. "Aw, that was nothing. Come on, all of us have our funny and embarrassing stories on the job. I even know one or two about you." She threw him a wink and kept pushing, the muscles in her legs straining.

The big man grinned. "That's good, I didn't mean to upset you. But something's eating at you. You want to talk about it?"

"Nah, I just got a lot on my mind, you know, stuff. Working out helps."

"It doesn't help enough." He lay a hand on her leg, stilling her. "You can't push your body so hard your mind stops, Chris. You of all people know that. Why don't you take it easy, take the rest of the day off? Go out, have some fun, get your mind straight."

She stopped and looked at him. "You sending me out the door, Chief?"

"No, nothing like that. You've just been putting a lot of time in lately. I went over your file, you've got some comp time to burn. And Joe would love to finish out the shift. You should take it off." He held up his hands innocently. "Just a suggestion. I think it would do you some good."

Chris looked at him, considering his words carefully. "Okay, maybe I could find something else to do today."

"Maybe?"

"Yeah, yeah, all right. I can. I'll take it off, just get off my ass, all right?"

He grinned at her. "That's the Chris I know and love! I'll go break it to Joe."

She smiled at his back as he walked away. *The Chris you know and love. Couldn't I just shock the shit out of you!* Her smile broadened as she walked over and picked up the phone.

The board chairman opened the door to the ambulance bay and leaned out. "We're ready for you now."

The crews all returned to the conference room and took their seats. The president announced Shelby as the supervisor and called the meeting to an end.

Shelby waited for the board members and the off-duty employees to leave, and then pulled Bryce, Cindy, and Fred aside.

"The scheduling system here sucks."

Fred nodded. "We all agree with you there."

"Fred, you've been here forever. Do you have any ideas on a new system?"

"I think I can come up with something."

"Great, I'm open to any ideas you might have. Cindy, I think you were thrown out on your own too early, and I want you to ride third for a while, learn the system better, and get some experience."

Cindy nodded, relief showing on her face.

"Bryce, partner up with Fred today. Help Cindy out, find out exactly what she knows, teach her what she doesn't. Okay?"

Bryce smiled almost as slowly as he drawled, "You got it, Boss. What are you gonna do?"

Shelby sighed. "Start on that office. I think Mike brought a tornado to help him get his stuff out."

Bryce laughed. "No, he always left it that way."

It was well after six when Bryce knocked on the office door. "Hey, Boss Lady, it's past quitting time. Pack it up and go home."

Shelby glanced at her watch. "Oh shit, Tori's got to be wondering where I am. I should call her."

"No, you shouldn't. Don't give her this news over the phone, go home."

"Bry, the work won't get done all by itself. Mike made such a mess out of this place. It's going to take me forever to get it straight."

He leaned in and looked at her. "You're beat. The mess will be here tomorrow. Go home. Go see your family."

She sighed. "You're right, as usual." She tossed the file she was working on into her briefcase, closed it, and stood up. "I'll see you in the morning."

"That's my girl. Let me walk you out."

Laura ran a hand through her hair and concentrated harder. Hannah sighed.

"Laura, ease up on yourself. You're a quick learner, but you're trying too hard."

Laura looked up at her. She was sitting cross-legged on the floor, mirroring Hannah's position, trying to learn her method of meditation. "No, I can get this, I really can. Just give me a minute."

Hannah reached out and took Laura's hands. "No, child. You're pushing yourself too hard. You can only do so much in a day, you'll exhaust yourself. Look how much you've learned today. You can't do any more. Go home."

Laura sighed. "I just want to learn it all, Hannah."

"And you will. But you can't learn it all today. Come on, give it a rest."

Laura stretched her neck, suddenly feeling tired. "Okay, if you say so."

"I do." Hannah smiled at her, the smile of a teacher with her favorite pupil. "Are you going to call Chris?"

Laura shook her head. "No, I don't think so. I think I want to figure me out before I throw myself into her."

Hannah patted her hand and got up. "Good choice. Now go home and rest. Tomorrow's another day."

"And another lesson."

"Or two, as fast as you're going through them!"

Chris walked quietly down the stairs, hoping the guys wouldn't notice her. As she reached the landing, Joe waved at her. She waved back, silently praying that she could get out the door before anyone else noticed her. Mark whistled.

"Hey, where are you going all dressed up?"

Shit. She put on a fake smile and turned around. "Out. I'll see you guys later."

A couple of the guys caught her before she reached the door. Mark walked a circle around her and whistled again.

"Wow, Chris. You clean up good! I almost didn't recognize you!"

I wish you hadn't. She smiled again. "Kiss my ass, Mark."

Mark stopped in his tracks. "Is that makeup? And leather pants? Oh, man, you just blew my whole image. What with that getup, I thought you were a girl till you opened your mouth. What the hell happened to you?"

"I am a girl, Mark, but another crack like that and I'll kick your ass worse than any man ever has."

Will reached out and touched her arm. "Ignore him, Chris, he's just jealous. I think you look great."

"Thanks, Will."

"You going out on a date or something?"

Her smile became genuine. "Something. I'm going to see a friend."

"You have a good time, okay?"

"Thanks, I'll do that."

The chief waved the guys back and escorted her out the front door. He waited for the door to close and turned to look at her. "Okay, what's this all about?"

"What do you mean?"

"This," he waved his hand at her. "It seems a little, I don't know, feminine, don't you think? Not really your style."

Chris laughed. "You don't think? You don't like it?"

"Oh, I like it. I'm just not sure you do. Does this have something to do with me sending you off today?"

"No, of course not." She sighed. "You're just not used to seeing me off duty. You may think I work like a man, but I really am a girl, you know."

The big man shook his head. "I know that. I just . . . Well, I worry about you. Like I would my own daughter."

"I'll be fine, Bob." She leaned over and kissed him lightly on the cheek. He blushed deep red, making her smile. "I appreciate your concern. And for the record, I love you, too."

She turned on her heel and walked away from him without looking back.

As soon as Shelby stepped through the door, Tori jumped up and hugged her.

"Where have you been? I was listening to the scanner and I didn't hear you running. I was starting to worry."

Shelby hugged her back. "I'm sorry, I got caught up in paperwork. It's been a long day, lots of news. But first, how was your day?"

Tori frowned, the man she and Ryan had given a speeding ticket to flickering through her mind. Then she shrugged.

"Just the usual group of idiots on the road. Tell me your news."

Shelby stood up straight and took a deep breath. "You are looking at the new supervisor of our local ambulance service."

"Oh, honey! I'm so happy for you! How'd this happen?"

"I'll tell you all about it, but first, do we have anything to eat? I forgot about lunch, and I'm starving."

"I saved supper for you. Let me heat it up."

Shelby followed Tori into the kitchen. "I saw Chris today."

"How is she?"

"I don't know, I didn't get a chance to talk to her. She's been acting funny lately. Kind of distant."

"I noticed that. I don't know what it's about." She set a plate down in front of Shelby. "Now tell me all about your promotion."

Shelby talked while she ate, telling Tori everything that had happened. Tori listened intently, pride welling up in her heart. She concentrated on Shelby, smiling and feeling good for her, but something still nagged at the back of her mind.

Chris took a deep breath and knocked softly. The door opened, and she felt her heart lighten at the sight of Laura. Laura smiled.

"Hello. What are you doing here?"

Chris lifted her hands, a bottle of wine in each one. "I wanted to replace these. I would have called first, but . . ." she shrugged.

Laura smiled again. "You didn't have to do that."

"I know. But I had ulterior motives. I wanted to thank you for last night. And I wanted to see you again." She shook her head. "Just to talk, I promise."

Laura opened the door wider. "Come on in."

Chris stepped into the apartment and took the wine to the kitchen. Laura followed her and reached into the cabinet for two glasses.

"So, did you need something, or are you just here to visit?"

Chris paused in pouring the wine. "I'm sorry. Is this a bad time?"

"Not at all." Laura reached over and touched Chris's hand so that she would resume pouring. "I just wondered."

Chris filled the glasses and set the wine bottle on the counter. "I know you're not sure about all of this, and I don't want to push you. I just wanted to see you."

Laura looked up at her and smiled. "I'm glad you came."

Chris followed Laura into the living room and sat uncomfortably on the edge of the sofa. Laura looked at her expectantly. Chris played with her glass nervously. *What the hell am I doing here? She didn't call; can't I take a hint?* "Laura, I think maybe last night . . . maybe I gave you the wrong impression. I don't want any discomfort between us. I just enjoy your company."

Laura set her glass on the coffee table. "I'm not uncomfortable. Are you?"

Chris shrugged. "No, I guess not. I just don't want you to get the wrong impression."

"What impression would that be?"

Chris took a sip of her wine. "That I want anything from you that you're not willing to give. I think I might have pushed you yesterday and I just want to . . . spend some time with you."

Laura smiled and picked up her glass. "I told you that you didn't. I wanted you to kiss me. I'm just not sure I'm ready to jump into bed with you." She stood, crossed the room, and turned on the stereo.

Soft guitar music filled the room. Chris looked up at Laura standing in front of her. Laura looked down and smiled, taking her hand gently. "No discomfort. No pressure. I kind of like being with you, too."

Chris sighed with relief and relaxed into the sofa.

Chapter Eight

Laura sat in her apartment and breathed deeply. She closed her eyes and took her mind further inside. Hannah's words echoed in her mind, but those words were beginning to sound less and less like Hannah's voice, and more like her own.

Find your center, wrap yourself around it. It is your core, the real you deep inside. You find that, and you've found your self, your true self, without all the outer trappings of the everyday.

She breathed deeply again and wrapped around her center. She held on, balancing, centering herself within the world. She felt that center balance, almost heard a click as it fell into place.

Now, Laura, and the voice was all her own now, *what is it you want in this life? What is it you need?*

The answer was almost an audible whisper.

Happiness. Love.

Love? What kind of love? Love of life? Love of someone else? Love of God?

All of these.

Love of life you have. Love of God you have. Love of someone else? Who?

It doesn't matter. Me, if need be.

Good. Love yourself first, then you can move on to love someone else.

Laura breathed deeply and smiled, opening her eyes. "Yes, I have to love me first. Find out what I want, and then move on from there."

"I don't have to listen to you! You're not my mother!" River stomped her foot to drive her words home.

Shelby stood facing her and forced her voice to be calm.

"I'm not trying to be your mother, River. But I am the other parent in this house, and you will listen to me."

Casey put his arm around his sister. "Come on, River, why are you doing this? Just go clean your room like Mom said. I'll help you."

"She's not my mom!"

"Yes, she is. Come on, I'll help you clean your room." Shelby watched as he turned his sister around and headed up the stairs. Erica went to her and hugged her.

"It's all right, Mom. She's just grouchy today. We still love you."

Today? Sometimes I think the child hates me. "I know, sweetheart. Now, you've got a room to clean, too."

"But I'm comforting you."

Shelby hugged the child. "And I love you for that, but it doesn't make you exempt."

Erica shrugged. "Can't blame me for trying!"

Shelby smiled as she watched Erica bound up the stairs two at a time. As soon as the children were all out of sight, she rubbed the back of her neck. *Oh, Tori, come home soon. I need you.*

"Hey, you."

Shelby whirled around to find Tori standing behind her.

"Hey."

"You look like you've had a rough day."

Shelby sighed. "You have no idea. River's at it again. I swear she hates me."

Tori unsnapped her duty belt and began pulling her uniform shirt off. "She does not. She's just rebelling; all kids do it."

"No, all kids don't do it, Tori. Just River. And I'm tired of it."

"Oh, come on, Shelby. It's not really that bad."

Shelby widened her eyes. "Not that bad! How would you know? You aren't seeing it. None of the kids do this to you."

Tori immediately went on the defensive. "Oh, so now your kids are perfect and mine aren't? Is that it?"

"No!" Shelby ran both hands through her hair. "Come on, Tor, we've never said 'yours' and 'mine.' That's not the way we are. I'm having a tough time, and I thought I could count on you to be there for me, to understand. I guess I was wrong."

Tori rolled her eyes. "Maybe you were."

Shelby headed for the door. Tori spun around and looked at her.

"Where are you going?"

"Out. I've been here all day and I need to get out for a while." She half turned, her hand on the doorknob. "Come with me."

"Shelby, I've been working all day, I just got here. I want to be home. Stay here with me."

"Why? So we can argue? I don't want to. I don't want this at all. I'm going out."

"Well, I'm staying home."

"Fine." Shelby stepped out the door and closed it behind her.

"Fine!" Tori yelled at the closed door.

*   *   *

Chris picked up the phone and dialed Laura's number. She hung up before it rang.

Chris, what the hell are you doing? She has your pager number, and did she call? No. She is not ready to admit who she is, and you can't be anyone else. You can't be seriously considering chasing this girl!

"But I am." Her voice rang out loudly in the empty apartment. She picked up the phone and started to dial again, changed her mind and slammed the phone back into its cradle. "Get her off your mind, Chris, get her off your mind any way you can." She stood up and paced through her apartment before grabbing her leather jacket and heading out the door.

Chris stepped in the door and saw Shelby sitting at the bar. She walked up and sat on the stool beside her.

"Hey, Shel, where's your better half?"

"Huh!" Shelby took a drink of her beer. Chris looked at her, concerned.

"What's going on?"

Shelby shook her head. "I don't know. Did you ever wake up one day and wonder how the hell you got there?"

Chris grinned. "All the time."

Shelby shook her head again. "Not like that. Like, how you got there in your life? What the hell are you doing? And what's the point? Isn't there something better out there somewhere?"

"All the time." Chris ordered a beer and turned to her. "But better than what? Your job? Your home? Tori and the kids? Is there any of that you could walk away from?"

Shelby sighed. "I don't know. Sometimes it just seems . . . old. Don't get me wrong, I love my kids, all of them. It's just that, sometimes I wonder."

"You wonder what? What it would have been like if

you hadn't made that choice? What it would be like without the burden?"

"No! The kids aren't a burden!"

Chris took a drink of her beer. "Tori, then. You wonder what it would be like without her?"

Shelby shrugged. "Maybe."

"You can't be serious."

"Why not? Look at you. You're single, happy. Getting it whenever you want. No ties, no responsibilities . . ."

Chris shook her head. "No responsibilities. No one to answer to. No one to go home to. No one who will be there no matter what. You really want my life?"

"It looks pretty good from where I sit. There's what, like three women in the world who wouldn't drop everything, give anything for one night with you. You can't tell me that's not an awesome feeling."

Chris turned on her stool and leaned her elbows on the bar. "Well, maybe it is. But from where you sit, you can't see the whole picture. You don't see the nights I spend alone in my apartment. You don't see what I see in you and Tori."

"And what's that?"

"Come on, you two are the poster girls for the perfect lesbian relationship."

Shelby took a long drink and let her breath out hard. "Poster girls. Posters are fake, you know. There's no such thing as perfect."

"But I see what you don't. I see the way she looks at you. She looks at you, and you're the only person in the world."

"And every other woman looks at you that way."

"But it's not the same. You look at Tori that way, too. I can't imagine feeling that much for anything. Anything that I have, anyway."

Shelby finished her beer. "I know, Chris. I'm just feeling a little . . . left out, I guess."

Chris hugged her friend. "Go home. Treasure what you have, don't look at the other side of the fence, the grass isn't any greener over here. It just looks good from a distance."

She hugged her back. "I know."

Chris waved her hand at Shelby and watched her leave. She picked up her beer and took a long drink, finished it and ordered another. A woman stepped up beside her and paid for it. She leaned close.

"Is your friend gone? Is this seat free?"

Chris shrugged. "Sure. Thanks for the beer."

The woman sat on the stool and crossed her long legs, looking at Chris. "Is there something wrong? Trouble with a lady?"

She laughed. "Ladies are no trouble. I've just got a lot on my mind, that's all."

"I could make you forget."

Chris looked at her. She was beautiful, her dark hair thick and wild, her blouse covering just enough to spark the imagination. Shelby's words echoed in her mind. *Every woman looks at you that way.* She smiled.

"I'm sure you could, but I'm not so sure your girlfriend would appreciate it." She indicated the redhead sitting next to the woman. The redhead stood up and stepped over to Chris. She leaned over her back and ran a hand softly down her arm.

"I think we could both make you forget. The question is, could you handle it?"

Chris chuckled. "Handling it isn't my worry, ladies. Work tomorrow is."

"Work?" The brunette cocked her head to one side and batted her eyes. "Is work really that important?"

"Yes, it is."

"What do you do?"

She smiled. "I'm a firefighter."

The redhead moved around to Chris's other side, sliding her breasts across her back as she went. "Firefighter? Now, that's hot. We've got a fire you could put out."

"I'll just bet you do. But I do have to work in the morning."

"Aw, we could get you to work on time. And make you forget whoever's on your mind. We promise."

Chris smiled and shook her head. "Ladies, I'm sure you could make anyone forget anything, at least for a while. But I don't think . . ."

They each pressed closer and the brunette leaned in, almost brushing her lips to Chris's. "What's wrong?" she whispered. "Too hot for you? Are you a one-woman girl?"

Chris lowered her eyelids and breathed in the woman's breath. "No, and obviously you aren't either."

The redhead leaned over and put her mouth close to theirs. "Nor am I."

The two women converged in a kiss, drawing Chris into their passion, both of them reaching out to her with their hands. Chris let her eyes close and allowed herself to be drawn into the kiss, drawn into the passion, thoughts of Laura pushed to the back of her mind for the first time in days.

Shelby lifted the covers and softly climbed into bed. She lay a moment in silence.

"You're home."

She jumped. "I didn't know you were awake."

"Of course I am. I don't sleep when you're not here."

Shelby rolled over and propped herself up on her elbow. "Tori, I'm sorry . . ."

"It's okay. I'm sorry, too." Tori rolled over and faced

her lover. "I talked to River. I think it's going to get better."

Shelby sighed. "God, I hope so. I'm sorry. I just get so frustrated sometimes."

"I know. And I do understand. She can be a tough kid to deal with."

Shelby reached over and touched Tori's face. "Like her mom."

"Hey! I'm not hard to deal with. I'm open to anything."

Shelby laughed. "Right up until you go into that cop mode. You clam up and get all defensive . . ."

Tori reached up and touched Shelby's lips, silencing her. "I don't like to argue, Shel."

"Me, either."

"But I must admit there is one perk to it."

"What's that?"

"The make-up sex is great." Tori kissed her.

"Oh," Shelby whispered. "And you think that sex will make everything all better?"

"Shh." Tori kissed her again. "You have the right"—she kissed her harder, and slipped her hand between Shelby's thighs—"to remain silent."

Shelby kissed her back, her breath coming in hard gasps, her hands reaching out and touching Tori, her body instantly responding to Tori's hands. Tori grinned and bit Shelby's lip playfully.

"Or scream if need be."

Shelby groaned and rolled over on top of Tori, giving her mind and body over to her lover, and taking hers in return.

Chapter Nine

Chris jumped out of the fire truck, eighty pounds heavier in all her gear. She turned to grab a hose line and felt the chief's hand land on her shoulder.

"Adams, we're not going in this one. Take a look."

She turned and focused on the house, quickly seeing what the chief was talking about. She reached behind her without looking and grabbed Will by his turnout coat, dragging him around beside her. "Will, what do you see?"

Will concentrated a moment, eyes locked on the small house. He saw smoke leaking out of the seams, around the windows and front door, under the eaves, then it was suddenly gone, sucked back in. He sucked in his own breath as he saw the walls of the house actually bulge.

"It's breathing. Backdraft conditions. We can't go in there."

Chris smiled. "Good boy. What are we going to do?"

"Timed horizontal ventilation. Has the walkaround been done?"

The chief nodded. "Can't use the front door; the window to the east will do fine, there's one in back, straight path through. Elvis, take Will and go around to the back, Mark and Jimmy will get the front, we'll push it toward you."

Chris glanced at the chief again. "I'd like to take Jimmy with me, I want Will up front."

He looked at her uneasily. "Are you sure? Will's never done this . . ."

"I'm sure, Chief. I'll put my life on it."

He nodded once and went to the firefighters who were laying out hose. Will turned to Chris.

"Hey, I don't know about this. Maybe Mark should—"

"You can do this, Will. I have faith in you," she interrupted. She leaned toward him, bumping her shoulder against his playfully. "Besides, I don't trust Mark to scrape the shit off my boots. I'd rather have my life in your hands, not his. I trust you."

Will took a deep breath. "Okay. I won't let you down."

She grinned and buckled up her turnout coat. "You'd better not! Run through it with me, tell me what we're doing."

"You and I will ventilate at the same time, keeping the fire inside."

"If you're too slow?"

"It'll explode on you."

"Good. We'll break through on one, Chief will count us down. Then what?"

"The attack team pushes the flames toward you, we contain inside the house, and douse it out."

She reached out and clapped him on the back. "Simple as that. No sweat. Ready?"

He nodded. "Yep."

Chris made her way carefully around to the back of the house, Jimmy close behind, always keeping one eye on the house. The walls bulged and caved in time with the smoke puffing out and sucking back in, breathing like a living thing.

Isn't it though? Isn't it a living thing? Maybe not the

house, but the fire is. It breathes, it eats, leaves waste behind. It can die. Doesn't that make it alive?

She stepped up to the window and hoisted her axe, enjoying the weight, the feel of it beneath her gloves. *Time to play.*

"Jimmy, you got my back?"

Jimmy stepped forward with his usual enthusiasm. "Right here, Elvis!"

"Then let's play!" She keyed the mike on her radio. "All set, Chief."

"Set here. It's a go. Bust on one," the chief's voice crackled back at her. She took a deep breath through her mask and tested the axe with a practice swing as she listened to him count.

"That's three, and two, and . . ."

His voice was lost in the sound of her swing hitting home, shattering the window, and the furious roar of the fire as the rush of air almost put it out. Chris instinctively rolled to her right as the attack team entered and doused the fire, pushing it toward her. By the time she was able to straighten up and look inside, the fire was down to smoldering ash. She yanked the mask off her face and turned to find Will running toward her with a grin that threatened to split his face wide open. She returned his grin and gave him a high five.

"I told you you could do it!"

"Hey, no sweat. I just wanted you to be sure."

"Liar." She cuffed his helmet and threw her arm around him as they made their way back around the house.

Shelby held out her left hand. "Cindy, a Miller four and an eight-oh tube."

Cindy stared at her.

Shelby looked up from the man she was working on.

"Cindy, I need to intubate this man. Give me the laryngo-scope with a Miller four-blade and an eight-point-zero tube, *now*."

Cindy blinked and reached for the airway bag. She fumbled with the zipper a moment. Bryce reached around her and plucked the bag out of her hands, deftly opening it and pulling out the equipment Shelby had asked for. He snapped the blade in place and slapped the handle into Shelby's outstretched hand. He pulled out a tube without looking, opened its packaging and put it in Shelby's other hand.

Shelby inserted the tube in the man's throat. Bryce slid the bag on the end of it and inflated the man's lungs. Shelby listened to his chest a moment and nodded. She taped the tube in place and looked at Bryce.

"Let's go, I'll do the rest en route."

Bryce nodded and jumped out the back of the ambulance. He climbed into the driver's seat and took off, siren wailing. Shelby looked at Cindy.

"You think you can bag?"

Cindy nodded, trying to keep the tears from welling up in her eyes.

"Good, take over. I need to get a line started."

Cindy moved around to the head of the man and took the bag in both hands. She squeezed. Shelby slid down the seat toward the man's arm. She wrapped a tourniquet around his arm and prepared to start an IV. She glanced at Cindy.

"Don't pull, you'll dislodge the tube. He's a bitch to in-tubate, I don't want to do it again."

Cindy nodded and concentrated on her job. Shelby looked back to her own work and slid the needle into the man's vein. She hooked up the IV tubing and taped it in place. Bryce called out to her, "You've got six to seven, Shel!"

Shelby reached over and picked up the radio mike. "EMS Seventeen, Doctor's Hospital ER, patient report."

The radio speaker crackled back at her, "Go ahead, Seventeen."

"Sir, en route to your facility, six to seven minute ETA, we have a seventy-three, seven-three-year-old male, no known history, no known allergies, patient was found unconscious approximately fifteen, one-five minutes ago, sporadic respirations." She let go of the transmit button and took a breath before pressing it again. "Patient is intubated, being bagged with high flow oh-two, pulse ox showing ninety-eight percent. Cardiac monitor showing SVT, rate of one twenty, one-two-zero, have IV established in left AC space with eighteen gauge, normal saline running TKO. Blood pressure is one ten, one-one-oh by palpation." She glanced up through the windshield as Bryce blew through a red light. "We now have approximately four minutes to you, do you have any orders or need anything further?"

"No further, EMS Seventeen, we'll be expecting you in four, see you in room two upon your arrival."

"Thank you, sir, EMS Seventeen clear."

Shelby snapped the mike back in its holder and recorded another EKG strip on the monitor. "Cindy?"

Cindy jumped. Shelby reached over and put her hand on Cindy's to keep her from dislodging the tube. "Just bag him."

"I'm sorry," Cindy's voice cracked. Shelby could tell she was near tears. She sighed.

"It's okay. We'll talk about it after we're done. Just bag him now, and don't fall apart on me."

Cindy swallowed hard and squeezed the bag, blinking back her tears.

The sun glinted off the bright red paint on the ladder truck, making Chris squint. She stepped back, a used wax rag in one hand, and looked over her work critically. Will stepped over to her.

"It looks good, Chris."

"Yeah, but you're the FNG, what do you know?" she teased.

Mark clapped him on the back. "She never lets up, man, never."

A car horn beeped behind them. They all turned around. Chris recognized the two women she'd met in the bar the night before as they smiled and waved at her. The redhead rolled down her window and called out to her, her ample bosom hanging out the car window.

"Hey, Chris, you working tonight?"

"Yep."

"Oh, too bad. Tomorrow?"

"Sorry, ladies, I can't do it."

She looked stricken. "Are you sure?"

Chris smiled. "Yeah, I'm sure. But, uh, I appreciate the offer."

"Well, you left something last night. You could come back for it if you change your mind . . ."

Chris smiled and waved as the window rolled up, and the women drove away. She turned back to the ladder truck. Will stood staring at her with his mouth open, Mark glowered.

"I told you, man, she's a menace. Us regular guys don't stand a chance when Elvis is around."

Will shook his head. "Did those girls just say you left something?"

Chris shrugged. "Yes, but I didn't. Hey, Mark, you want to back that one in and pull out the rescue unit? We'll wax it while we're at it."

Mark climbed in the ladder truck and fired it up. Will looked at her and scratched his head.

"Oh, tell me you didn't do what I think you just did."

"What's that, Will?" She watched Mark back the truck in and climb in the other one.

"You blew them off!"

Chris turned and smiled at him sweetly. "No, blowing doesn't really come into play in my life."

"You know what I mean! You turned them down!"

She shrugged. "So?"

"But they . . . they wanted . . . are you nuts?"

Chris looked at him, suddenly serious. "No, Will, I'm not nuts. Just tired. They all want the same thing, every single one of them. It's all about sex. I'm tired of the whole scene."

He looked incredulous. "But . . . two beautiful women just wanted you to . . . to . . . I can't believe you *turned that down*. How can you possibly get *tired* of that?"

"Why wouldn't I?"

"Be . . . because . . . they . . ." he stuttered and shook his head. "It's everyone's fantasy! How could you not want that?"

"What, sex with a couple of beautiful women?" She sighed and shook her head. "You know, I've been there and done that. There's more to life."

"More? Like what?"

"Like something that touches you above the waist, Will. Something more than just sex, something that stimulates your mind, your . . ."

She suddenly stopped and stood staring at the rescue truck Mark had pulled out. *Heart. Something that stimulates your mind and your heart. There is more to life. That's it! That's what's been going on in my head! That's why I can't seem to get satisfied. They couldn't do it last night, God knows they tried. And that's why I turned down the woman in front of the bookstore the other day.*

Because I need more. I want more. I want Laura. That's why I can't get her out of my head. Because she is more. She makes me think, she makes me feel.

She walked into the station, tossed her wax rag in the corner and picked up the phone. She dialed the number to the bookstore from memory. Laura picked up.

"Hello, Celestial Dreams."

"Hi, Laura, this is Chris." There was silence on the other end. "Laura, are you there?"

"Yes, I'm here. I just didn't expect . . . I didn't think you'd call."

"I know, I'm sorry. Are you busy? I could call back later."

"No, not at all. What's on your mind?"

"You." *She sounds so confident, so . . . together. Is this the wrong thing to do? She didn't call me, maybe she wasn't interested after all.* "I just . . . I'd like to talk to you. I'd like to see you. I'm sorry, I'm not very good at this. I'd like to explain . . . I'd like to . . . I don't know, see you."

"Okay."

"Is tomorrow evening all right? We could go out somewhere . . ."

"Why don't you just come by my place?"

Chris nodded, holding the phone tightly. "I could do that."

"Around eight?"

She nodded again. "I'll be there."

"Okay."

"Okay. So I'll see you then."

"Okay. Bye."

"Bye." Chris hung up the phone and sighed, wiping a hand across her forehead.

* * *

Tori sighed as she climbed back into her cruiser. Ryan looked at her.

"Something wrong, Partner?"

"Not really."

"Not really, but maybe? Come on, you've been moping all day. Not getting enough at home?"

Tori laughed. "Enough of what? Enough of Shelby fighting with River? Enough of trying to fix everything, make it all all right again? God, ten years and sometimes I still don't know what's going on in her head!"

"Who, Shelby?" He pulled back into traffic. "Shelby loves you. Why do you need to know what's in her head? Let it go, it'll work out."

"I don't know. I keep telling myself it will, but I just don't know."

"Are you kidding? You're not considering . . ."

"No, I'm not going to leave her. I couldn't, I love her."

"Then what are you getting at?"

"I don't know. I guess I just didn't realize that relationships were this much *work*, you know? I mean, you go into it thinking it's the greatest, most exciting thing that has ever been. Then one day you wake up and realize that you're *comfortable*."

"Comfortable is good."

Tori looked out the window. "I guess so. I just miss the excitement sometimes."

Ryan shrugged. "So bring back some of that excitement."

"How? It's not like you can go out and pick it up and bring it home. It's not like you can open a bottle of it and get your lover interested. It takes two to stop the fighting long enough to get excited."

"You're fighting?"

"Well, not really fighting. Just having arguments."

"Well, if you're fighting, then obviously the passion is still there. And do you make up after the arguments?"

Tori laughed out loud. "Oh, yes. The make-up sex is fantastic! Sometimes I wonder if I argue with her just to get it!"

"That good, huh?"

"Better!"

"Damn! Maybe I should start a fight with David!"

Tori laughed harder. "David wouldn't fight with you. He'd just say 'yes sir' and do whatever you wanted. You big old butch man, you!"

Ryan ducked his head and blushed. "Yeah, he'd like it though!"

Tori pointed the radar gun at a fast-moving car. "There's one."

Ryan nodded and flipped on the siren as he pulled away from the slower traffic and began the chase.

Shelby stepped out of the ER doors and looked in on Bryce waiting for her in the ambulance. She checked the back; everything was in order, but something was missing.

"Where's Cindy?"

Bryce pointed to the corner of the building, where the employees sometimes went to smoke out of sight. Shelby sighed and headed in that direction. She rounded the corner and found Cindy, just lighting up. Cindy offered her one. Shelby took it, lit up, and looked at Cindy.

"Cindy, do you like it here with us?"

"I screwed up again, didn't I?"

Shelby sighed. "It's not so much that. It's just that, well, you don't seem to be getting it."

"I know." She looked at Shelby, her eyes pleading. "I'll try harder, I really will."

"It's not a matter of trying, Cindy. I know you're trying, everybody knows that. I couldn't ask you to try more. I just don't think trying is always enough."

Cindy hung her head, her eyes filling with tears. "You're going to get rid of me, aren't you?"

Shelby raked her fingers through her hair. "I don't want to, I really don't. Your skills are good, and your bedside manner is fantastic. And you have more heart than most people I know."

"But that's not enough."

"No, I'm afraid it's not."

"But I love EMS. I love helping people. It's what I want to do."

Shelby reached out and put a hand on Cindy's arm. "I know you do. And I'm not getting rid of you. I just want you to look at other options. There are other ways to help people, besides working on the streets."

Cindy crushed out her cigarette. "Other options. Like what?"

"Well, your office skills are great, you could find something related there. Like billing or office management."

Cindy shook her head. "I couldn't. I'm good at that stuff, but I hate it. I need contact with people. I could never work in an office. I'd go crazy."

"Okay, scratch that. What about the ER? You'd still be doing direct patient care, still in Emergency, but in a more controlled environment. You would still be doing your skills, still be involved with the people. You just wouldn't have to be on scene, out of your environment. That's where you seem to have your problems."

Cindy shrugged. "I don't know."

"Or, there's always Dispatch."

"Oh, no. Dispatch doesn't do anything!"

Shelby raised her eyebrows. "Really? Do you think we'd be out here without them? They do an amazing amount of work. Most systems won't even consider you for the position unless you have at least two years experience as a street medic. It's a promotion."

Cindy wrinkled her nose. "Why?"

"Because they do so much. They take care of all of us on the street, they give callers instructions before we get there, and they get us all the help we need. And they do that for every ambulance in the area at the same time, plus they track the birds. You've never been in there?"

Cindy looked at Shelby, wide-eyed, and shook her head.

"We'll go by there today, Cappy's on. You see if he doesn't do anything."

"Cappy?"

Shelby nodded. "He used to be a captain over at the fire department. He moved into Dispatch about seven years ago, after an injury. He tells me the job's a lot harder than firefighting ever was."

"Really?" Cindy sounded hopeful.

"Yes, really. Come on, we'll go over there. If nothing else, you should at least know how they run the place."

Shelby clapped her on the back and turned her toward the ambulance.

Chapter Ten

Shelby saw Tori waving them in as Bryce pulled into the drive. The house was big, two stories, with a wrought-iron fence and manicured hedges.

Domestic abuse has no boundaries.

Tori met Shelby as she climbed out of the ambulance. "Hey, Shel. This one's pretty bad, bruised up, maybe a dislocated shoulder."

Shelby shook her head. "Is she going to press charges?"

"He. And I don't think so. Ryan's trying."

Shelby raised her eyebrows. "He? There's a twist."

"Not really, we've been out here several times; this guy just can't seem to get enough. He probably wouldn't have even called, but she left, so he thought it might be safe."

As Tori led her into the house, Shelby noticed the plush carpeting, the expensive furniture, the walls covered with art. She could almost smell the money that went into creating the atmosphere. *No, domestic abuse has no boundaries. Not money, race, class, age. Not even gender. God, how does society breed these people?*

Tori led Shelby into a room that looked like an office. The man sat in an overstuffed leather chair, holding a towel to his bleeding face with one hand, shaking his head slowly at Ryan, his other arm hanging at an angle that Shelby recognized. She almost cringed before putting on her smile and stepping up to the man.

"Sir, can you tell me what happened?"

The man looked up at her with one eye that pleaded for her to believe him. "I fell down the stairs."

She nodded as she crouched before him, gently taking his arm. "How many flights? Just one?" She carefully manipulated his arm to a crooked position and held it against his chest, lifting a little to alleviate the pressure on his shoulder.

"Ahh, yes, just one flight. Oh, that's better. Do you think it's okay? Is it dislocated?"

"No, sir, I think your clavicle is broken. Do you hurt anywhere else Mister . . ."

"Thomas. Daniel Thomas. Just my shoulder and my face. I kind of have a headache." He dropped the towel from his face.

Shelby closed her eyes for a second. *He doesn't have any idea. God, what did she do, hit him with a steel bar?* She glanced beside her. "Cindy, take c-spine will you please?" She turned back to her patient and smiled again. "Mr. Thomas, please hold your head very still for me okay?" She reached over and touched the orb of the man's eye that had been covered by the towel. She felt the shattered bones as he cringed back.

"I got a pretty good shiner there, huh?"

"I think it's a lot worse than that, Mr. Thomas. Will you go to the hospital with me?"

"Do you think that's necessary? I'd really rather not, if I have a choice."

"Well, you do have a choice. I can't make you go, but I think it is necessary. I'm not a doctor, and I don't have X-ray eyes, but I think you have some broken bones that are going to need treatment."

"Really? Broken?" He sounded doubtful. "I just thought

my shoulder was dislocated; it feels a lot better in this position."

"Not really your shoulder, your clavicle. It's this bone right here." She touched his uninjured shoulder. "It holds your shoulder up, that's why it feels better when I lift it. I'm much more concerned about this eye. I think you've broken the bones around it, and that's going to require surgery. Will you let me take you to the hospital?"

He frowned. "If you think I should go."

She nodded. "Guys, I want him on a board." Bryce clapped Ryan on the shoulder and they turned to go out to the ambulance. Shelby noticed Cindy's fingers start to move and looked up at her. "Cindy, you stay there and hold. Tori, will you help me with a triangle?"

"Sure." Tori rummaged in the trauma bag and came up with the cloth bandage. Shelby held his arm while Tori made a sling and tied it in place. Shelby slid her hands out just as Bryce and Ryan came back in with the stretcher loaded down with equipment. The five of them made quick work of backboarding the man and wheeling him out to the ambulance. Shelby leaned out the back doors and spoke to Tori.

"Hey, you know where the wife is?"

Tori nodded. "We've got a pretty good idea, but we can't touch her if he won't press charges."

"You won't even pick her up?"

"We can't, Shelby, you know that."

Shelby shook her head disdainfully. "Sometimes your job sucks." She leaned back in her ambulance and pulled the doors closed behind her.

Tori rolled her eyes. "Never more than when you bitch about it."

Ryan looked at her doubtfully. "You guys okay?"

Tori sighed. "Same old, same old. You know."

"Yeah, I know." But he looked at her worriedly as she

climbed back into their cruiser and motioned for him to hurry.

Shelby looked down and patted her patient's hand. "All right, Mr. Thomas, we'll get you taken care of." She glanced at Cindy.

"Cindy? This one's all yours. What do you want?"

Cindy stared at her, wide-eyed. "Um, I think I need a blood pressure."

Shelby nodded. "Good, start there."

She watched Cindy as she wrapped the cuff around the man's uninjured arm and pumped it up. Cindy listened, her eyes on the gauge as she let the air out slowly. She pursed her lips and tried again, letting the air out of the cuff even more slowly and watching the gauge. She took the stethoscope out of her ears, shaking her head.

"I can't hear anything. I can see it bounce, but I can't hear it."

Shelby slid over beside her, picked up Cindy's hand and placed her fingers on the man's wrist. "Then palpate it. You feel the pulse?"

Cindy nodded.

"Okay, now watch the gauge, and mark when you can feel it again. I'll listen." She put her own stethoscope in her ears and placed it on the man's arm, pumping the cuff up again. She listened as she slowly let the air out, watching the gauge. She clearly heard the steady thump-thump of the blood pumping through the man's veins. When the sound faded, Shelby let the rest of the air out of the cuff and turned to Cindy. "What'd you feel?"

"I got pulse back at one twenty."

"Good, I had one twenty-six over sixty-eight, so you're doing fine."

"I don't know how you could possible hear that, with all the noise in here."

Shelby smiled. "Practice, honey. I've been doing this almost as long as you've been alive. Now what?"

Cindy glanced through the windshield. "We've got what, fifteen minutes to go?"

Shelby nodded. "Time enough to do whatever you want. What's next?"

"Um," she glanced around, as if looking for answers written on the walls of the box they were in. "He's already splinted. I need a history."

Shelby nodded. *That should have been done already, honey. God, is she ever going to get this?* "Yes, you do. Go ahead, I'll be right here beside you if you need anything." She picked up a pad and started jotting notes as the man answered Cindy's stumbling questions. *No, I'm not sure she will ever get this. God help us all.*

Chris knocked softly on Laura's door. Laura opened it, and Chris stepped in to find the apartment bathed in golden candlelight. Soft music was playing and Laura stepped into her arms and kissed her.

"That's some welcome. What did I do to deserve it?"

"Just being you."

"Well, I'll have to be me more often."

"Be serious."

Chris nodded. "I can do serious."

"I want you, Chris."

"I want you, too, Laura. I just . . . I want you to be sure."

"I am sure. Can't you see that?"

"No, I can't. Can we sit down, talk for a minute?"

"Sure." Laura led her to the sofa and sat beside her. Chris sighed heavily and took Laura's hands in hers.

"I'm just scared, Laura."

Laura raised her eyebrows in surprise. "You?"

"Yeah, me. I suddenly realized a few things yesterday,

that's why I called you. I realized that I've been doing everything I can do to get you off my mind. And it's not working."

"Well, that's good."

She smiled. "Maybe. But that's what scares me."

"Why? I can't get you off my mind, and it doesn't scare me. Not anymore."

"No?"

"No. I've gotten past the fear and I found something else. Something better. Why does it scare you?"

"Because . . . because you've opened a door. A door in my heart. One that I closed a long time ago. One that I didn't ever think would be opened again."

"Tell me. Tell me why you closed that door."

"Because I won't be hurt. But in order not to let in hurt, you have to close the door on your feelings. If you can't feel, you can't hurt."

Laura looked at her with adoration and sympathy. "She really broke your heart, didn't she?"

"Yes, she did."

"And you really loved her."

Chris nodded. "Yes, I did."

"Do you still?"

"No."

"Then tell me about her."

Chris sighed. "It was a long time ago, Laura. A very long time ago. I was young and foolish. I fell in love."

"Falling in love is good."

"Not if she's straight. I fell in love, and I was convinced that she felt the same way. I thought love could keep her. I was wrong."

"She left you?"

"I couldn't give her what she needed. I thought love could cross all boundaries. But it couldn't, and she couldn't stay with me. She was straight, and I couldn't change that."

"But if she was with you, how could she be straight? I don't get it."

"I guess she thought she'd changed. I sure thought so. But eventually, she decided that this life wasn't for her."

"She went back to men?"

"Yes, she did. I heard she got married, had a couple of kids. I think she fights for Reforming the Queers or some other shitty organization like that. I don't know."

"So now you won't touch a woman who's not a dyed-in-the-wool born lesbian."

Chris laughed. "That's the funny part. I do. I think I gravitate toward them. I've had more so-called straight women than you could imagine. I don't know why, maybe to prove that I can, maybe for spite, I don't know. But I never let them in. I keep everything that's really me hidden. I built this wall, and I don't ever go outside of it. I have sex with women, one night stands, maybe short flings, but I don't talk to them. Until I met you. Now, I actually want to talk. I want to spend time with you. I don't want those other women anymore. I just want you."

"Good. Because I want you, and no one else."

"And that brings us here."

"Yes, it does." She leaned in as if to kiss her. Chris pulled back.

"But how do you know? You've never been with a woman. How do you know?"

"Because I know. I know who I am, and what I want. I don't care if you're a woman or a man, I just want to be with *you*."

"How do you know? You weren't so sure when we met."

"I've been soul-searching. Hannah has helped, but it's my soul, my heart. And I've found it." Laura leaned over and kissed her.

Chris kept her eyes closed after the kiss and whispered, "I'm scared, Laura. I'm scared of you. I'm scared that if I let you in, I'll get hurt."

Laura reached up and touched Chris's face with one hand, burying the other in her honey hair as she whispered back, "I won't hurt you, love. I won't hurt you."

Laura kissed her again and Chris felt her body heat rise. She was amazed that any woman could make her feel this way with only a kiss. Chris let the feeling flow over her, picked up the smaller woman and carried her to the bedroom. She lay her on the bed and slowly undressed her, marveling at the softness of her skin. She could feel Laura trembling, and her own excitement rose.

Laura reached out and tugged Chris's shirt out of her jeans, running her hands along her bare back. Chris inhaled sharply, trying to control her own desire at the touch of Laura's hands.

"You're trembling, Laura. Are you afraid?"

Laura bit her bottom lip. "Not really, maybe a little nervous." She brought her hand up to Chris's face, one finger tracing the wide line of her jaw, the arch of her eyebrow. "But this is what I want."

"You're sure? Really sure?"

"Yes. More sure than I've ever been about anything."

Laura closed her eyes as Chris touched her. She felt the trails of fire left on her skin by Chris's fingertips, the way her body responded to Chris's touch, opening up to every possibility.

One last coherent thought lingered in her mind as she was lost in the emotion that overwhelmed her.

This is what I was put on earth for.

Chapter Eleven

The sound of the sirens winding down outside her building pulled Laura out of the book she was reading. She looked out her third-story window and saw a fire truck, two police cruisers, and an ambulance pull up across the street. She couldn't see any smoke. She looked closer and noticed the workers all moving around, looking up. She followed their gaze and saw a man on the ledge of the building across from her, two stories higher.

Laura was close enough to the workers to be able to distinguish the different people. She watched them put their heads together. Suddenly, they all turned and looked at one firefighter. Laura followed their gaze again and watched as the firefighter began to strip off gear. As the coat and helmet were removed and handed off to another firefighter, she realized it was Chris.

Chris razzed her chief as she stripped off her turnout gear. "This isn't a firefighter's job, Chief. Isn't there a cop somewhere that does this kind of stuff?"

He nodded. "The negotiator. It's going to take twenty minutes to get him over here. We need someone to go up there and keep this guy calm until then."

"Come on, Chief, you got plenty of guys on this crew with the balls to go up there."

"Sure, I got plenty of 'em. But you're the only one with the balls and the training. So that makes you the best man for the job."

"Yeah, I hear that a lot." *But I've never been worried about it before. Why am I now?*

"Hey, Adams." The chief leaned close to her, his face lined with worry.

"Yeah, Chief?"

"He's one of the brotherhood."

Her eyes widened and she looked up. "One of ours?"

The chief nodded. "He was with the Department about fifteen years ago. We lost a couple guys in an arson fire, and he saw it all. He just couldn't go back in after that."

She looked at the chief, then back up at the man on the ledge. "That's why you want me up there."

He nodded. "If anyone can get to him, it's you. His name is Nick."

"Nick."

"And Chris, bring him back for us. He was a good firefighter once, I'd hate to see him end this way."

She walked slowly to the rescue truck and tossed her gear inside, trying to get her thoughts together. She chanced a quick look at the gathering crowd, realizing that she was looking for Laura.

Stop it, Chris. Get your mind on the job. She glanced up at the windows of the apartment building across the street, Laura's apartment building. *Is she there, watching me?* She sighed as she walked back toward the building, going inside and climbing the stairs to the fifth floor.

God, Chris, stop! You know better than this! A firefighter with something else on her mind is going to get killed. Or worse, get someone else killed.

She emerged on the right floor and someone directed her to the open window. She leaned out slowly, avoiding any sudden movements. The man had climbed out the window and moved several feet away, along the narrow ledge. He was standing with his back against the building, swaying back and forth. He suddenly turned toward her, swaying farther out.

"Get away from me! I'll jump!"

Chris put her hands out. "Hey, take it easy. I'm just here to talk, okay?"

He shook his head violently, making him lean out. "No, you're not. You're here to stop me, I know how you people work."

"Stop you? No, man, I'm just here to find out why you're here."

He paused, looking at her. "What do you care?"

Chris shrugged. "I care."

"No, you don't."

She shrugged and pulled herself through the window. She sat on the edge, her back to the empty office, her feet dangling high above her crew. She glanced down and saw them looking up at her. She caught herself glancing at the building across the street and forced herself to look back to the man on the ledge. "Okay, maybe I care and maybe I don't. But I need to know why you're up here."

"Why?"

Chris knew the man was stalling, knew he didn't want to jump. *It doesn't matter now what you talk about, just keep talking. That's all he needs, time to think this through.*

She indicated the growing crowd with a wave of her hand. "Well, you didn't leave a note, did you?"

"What?"

"You know, a note. For those people down there. For your family, your friends." She indicated the office behind her. "The people you work with. They'll want to know why you did it. And my chief seems to think he knows you."

"Screw them." The man looked down and turned back to her. "You're with Bobby's department?"

She nodded. "Yeah. But screw them. Maybe I'll just come out there and join you."

He looked at her in astonishment. "You don't want to do that."

"Why not? You are."

"That's different."

"Why?"

"You wouldn't understand."

She stood up. "Try me."

Laura watched Chris from her window, reading glasses perched on the end of her nose, book forgotten in her lap. *Oh my God, she's going up there!* She held her breath until Chris appeared in the window, close to the man on the ledge. *No, she's not! Oh, God, no.*

Laura watched Chris pull herself through the window and sit on the ledge, feet dangling. Time slowed to a crawl for Laura as she watched her lover get up and inch her way along the ledge. *This isn't happening. I'm just imagining this because this is* not *happening.*

But it was. And she was watching. She couldn't stop. She watched Chris inch her way slowly to the man. It occurred to her that she should be proud. Her lover was risking her life to save someone else, she should be proud. She wasn't. She was afraid.

She could tell Chris and the man were talking, but she wasn't close enough to tell what they were saying. She watched the man rub his eyes and shake his head, and Chris reached out to him.

God, just get away from him. She didn't even realize

she was chewing her fingernails. *He's crazy, Chris, just get away from him. Oh, God, this isn't happening.*

Chris reached out her hand. The man looked at it, then at her, tears spilling from his eyes.

"I-I can't."

"Yes, you can. I'm right here. I'm right here with you."

He reached out and took her hand, gripping tightly. "I'm afraid."

She nodded. "It's okay to be scared. It's okay. I've got you."

Laura watched Chris hold out her hand, watched the man take it. She watched as they slowly made their way back to the window. Only when they climbed back inside did she let out the breath she hadn't been aware she'd been holding. She got up and went to the kitchen, shakily pouring herself a glass of wine.

Chris glanced at her watch as she watched the ambulance pull away, the man from the ledge on board. *Another thirteen hours left.* She looked up, hoping to see Laura looking out one of the windows above her, hoping she wouldn't. The chief walked up and clapped her on the back.

"Good job, Adams. One for the books."

She rolled her eyes. "Yeah, another one. Hey, Chief, I'm a firefighter, remember? Not a damn monkey. Next time you go up, huh?"

He laughed. "I told you, you're the best man for the job."

"Best woman, Chief."

He eyed her appreciatively. "That, too."

She smiled at his joke, but her smile faded as she climbed back into her truck. She gazed out the window, thinking of Laura. *Thirteen hours before I can see her again. This is going to be on the news, she'll be worried. I'll call her when I get back to the station.*

One of the guys leaned over and pushed his shoulder against hers. "Hey, you were great up there."

She tipped her head but didn't say anything. He leaned closer.

"You okay?"

She sighed, still thinking of Laura. "Yeah, I'm okay."

"You don't look okay."

Chris turned to him, her grin feeling fake and stiff on her face. "I'm just getting too old for this shit."

Shelby walked in the front door and headed straight for the den. She deposited her books on her desk and sighed, rubbing her neck with one hand. Tori stepped up behind her.

"Rough day, love?"

Shelby turned and wrapped her arms around her lover. "Oh, if you only knew."

Tori held her in return. "Enlighten me."

"Oh, it's just everything at once. This EMT class is getting to the part where I'm going to start losing people. And Cindy, God help me with her."

"Cindy? Your rookie EMT? She's still not working out?"

Shelby let go of Tori and ran a hand through her hair. "No, she's not. And it's sad, you know. She has all the heart in the world, she loves her job. She just sucks at it. I don't know if she had a bad example set for her, or if she just can't do it. I feel like Bryce and I are just dragging her along. And you know how busy we've been. Now we're headed for the night rotation." She turned around and picked up Tori's beer, helping herself to a long draught.

"And just when I thought I had all of Mike's mess cleaned up, I opened up the computer files. What a nightmare!"

"I'm sorry, love. I can't help you there."

"I know. Believe me, if you could help, I'd put you to work."

"But at least you get to come home."

Shelby rolled her eyes and took a deep breath. Tori furrowed her brow.

"What? Coming home's not good?"

"Yes, honey, of course it is. It's just . . . not so easy here, either."

Tori groaned. "Oh, no. Is River at it again? I thought she quit that."

"I wish." Shelby shook her head and turned away from her lover. "I don't know what to do, Tor. I've tried everything I can think of. She doesn't respond to me. I don't get it. She used to. She was my best buddy, remember?"

Tori nodded and ran her hands down Shelby's arms. Shelby leaned her head back on Tori's shoulder. "I just don't know what happened. I've lost her, and I don't even know why, much less how to fix it."

Tori kissed her temple. "I'll talk to her again. Maybe I can do something."

Shelby put on her best that's-been-tried-before-but-go-ahead smile and sighed. "I think I just need a break. A good old break, where I can forget everything for a while. Get out of reality."

"A break, huh?" Tori grinned and slipped her hands around Shelby's torso, resting them on her hips. "Our weekend is coming up soon, that'll give you a break."

"It can't happen soon enough!"

"So, you need a break. Is that all you need?"

Shelby turned around and wrapped her arms around Tori, kissing her softly. "That's all."

Tori grinned and kissed her neck. "Nothing else?"

Shelby leaned her head back and closed her eyes as Tori nipped her neck. "No, nothing else. Nothing I can think of."

Tori turned Shelby's back to her desk and lifted her a little, sitting her on the desk. She pulled Shelby's shirt over her head and ran her hands up and down her body. "Nothing else? Nothing I can help you with?" She kissed her again.

Shelby gave in to the kiss, wrapping her legs around Tori and plunging her fingers into her hair. "Nope, don't think you can help me."

"No?" Tori continued the game. Her hand found Shelby's crotch and she leaned into her harder as she rubbed. "Well, in that case, I guess . . ." she breathed heavily as she kissed Shelby again. "I'll just leave you alone then."

Shelby returned Tori's kiss, her eyelids dropping and her neck rolling back. "Well, maybe there's just a little something. . . ." She reached out and pulled off Tori's shirt. Tori stepped back, letting Shelby slide off the edge of the desk. Shelby grabbed her and kissed her again.

"You might be able to help me out with a little something . . . upstairs."

Tori grinned as Shelby took her hand.

"Hello?"

Chris smiled at the sound of Laura's voice on the phone. "Hi."

"Oh, God, Chris." Laura suddenly sounded breathless. "I was so worried about you! You scared the hell out of me up on that ledge!"

"Oh, no need to worry about me." Chris smiled in spite of her calming words. *She worries about me. I think I like that.* "I'm always fine."

"But I wasn't! I was watching you, and it scared me to see you up there with that nut. Weren't you scared?"

Chris shrugged. "Maybe a little. But it's nothing I haven't done before, and probably will again."

"Oh, don't! Don't do that again!"

"Laura, I have to. This job is a part of who I am, I can't change it."

Laura sat silent a moment. Chris put some cheer in her voice and changed the subject. "Hey, want to go away with me?"

"Away?"

"Yes. There's this weekend that we do every year, a whole bunch of us . . ."

"Oh, the Pride weekend?"

"How'd you know?"

"Oh, I've heard the stories."

Chris laughed. "Lies, all lies! Whatever they told you, it's not true! I would never do such a thing!"

Laura laughed back. "I don't think so! Hannah wouldn't lie to me!"

"Hannah told you?"

"Yes."

"Shit!" Chris grinned. "Then I guess I'm in trouble!"

"No, you're not. Just don't think it'll be the same with me there!"

"So you'll go with me?"

"Of course I will. If last night wasn't a one night stand."

Laura had to strain to hear Chris's whispered reply. "No. One night isn't enough." She cleared her throat and spoke up. "And you're ready for that? The Pride weekend?"

"Why wouldn't I be?"

"Well, I just wasn't sure. With you being new to this lifestyle and everything, you know. I don't want to throw you into anything too fast."

Laura smiled. "I'm ready. I told you, I've been finding out a lot about myself lately, and I'm sure."

"Okay, if you're sure. And there are a couple other things we do every so often. I'd love it if you'd come with me."

"Like what?"

"Oh, there's a training weekend we do every year, one long party in the woods. And another Pride weekend, and every two or three years Tori, Shelby, and I go on a two-week vacation. Something wild like snowboarding in the Rockies, or sailing the Pacific."

Laura smiled. *Long-term plans. No, I guess it wasn't a one night stand.* "Are you guys nuts?"

"Maybe. But I'd like you to come be nuts with us. You'll love Shelby and Tori, really. They're great. And if you're free next Sunday, you can meet everybody then."

"What's next Sunday?"

"Karaoke night."

"Karaoke night? Now I know you're nuts!"

"No, really, it's a blast. A bunch of us spend the day together, doing something weird, then we all go out to Karaoke that night."

"A bunch of us? Who's us?"

"Firefighters, cops, EMTs, paramedics, a couple of nurses. Just friends. Family."

"Sounds like a big family."

"It's kind of funny. It seems like, if you've been out for a while, all your friends are gay. They become a family to you. But in this business, we're all a family. Those of us who work together. These guys at the firehouse, they're my brothers. I have to be able to count on them for my life, and they count on me. We don't just work together. We live together half the time. They are my family, too. Does that make sense?"

"I guess it does."

Chris took a deep breath. "So I'd like you to meet them."

"Okay."

"Is Sunday good for you?"

"Sure, it sounds like fun. I can't wait. So, when do I get to see you again?"

"I don't get off until tomorrow. You'll be at work."

"You could come by on your way home."

"Yes, I could. I will. And how about dinner after work tomorrow? I know this great steak house across town . . ." Sensing a silence on the other end of the line, she stopped. "Laura?"

"Um, I'm here."

"What's wrong? Did I say something?"

"No, it's nothing, really. It's just, I guess you wouldn't know, would you?"

Chris felt her heart sink into the pit of her stomach. "Know what?"

"I'm a vegetarian. I don't eat steak."

Chris let out a long breath as relief washed over her. "Is that all? You had me worried for a minute there. I thought it was something serious."

"It is. I haven't eaten meat in six or seven years. I don't mind if you do, but I won't."

"Oh, no, that's fine. I didn't mean to imply that it wasn't serious, I just thought you meant something that would keep us apart."

She could hear the smile in Laura's voice. "I'll see you in the morning then."

"Okay. Hey, Laura?"

"Yes?"

"If you want anything before then, just page me, okay? I'll call you back as soon as I can."

"Okay, I'll do that."

"Okay, great. I'll see you in the morning."

"Yeah." *I love you.* Laura stopped the words before they came out of her mouth. *You'll scare her away for sure.* "I'll see you in the morning."

Chris smiled as she hung up the phone. *I'll have to talk to Shelby. God, I think I'm falling in love with this woman.*

Chapter Twelve

Tori slowly raised her head until her eyes were peeking over the wooden crate she was using for cover. She lifted her rifle and lined up the sights. She kept her eye on her target and slowly squeezed the trigger.

Joe saw Tori aiming at him too late and tried to duck. Her shot hit him square in the chest, knocking him off his feet. He lay sprawled, looking at the red stain on the front of his shirt.

"Damn, Tori, do you have to pump it up so high? You'd think you were trying to kill me!"

Tori barely glanced at him as she ran, crouching, to the next cover crate. She aimed again, this time at Shelby. Shelby ducked behind her own crate and returned fire. She missed, hitting instead the corner of Tori's cover at an angle, splashing yellow paint onto her face shield.

Laura watched the game from a balcony overlooking the paintball arena. Susan sidestepped to her, leaned on the railing and pointed.

"She's over there, behind that post, stalking Bryce."

Laura followed Susan's finger with her eyes, spotting Chris hiding behind a post. She shook her head in bewilderment. "They're like animals, hunting each other. I don't get it."

Susan laughed. "Obviously. You didn't last long."

They both glanced down at Laura's clothes, splattered with three different colors of paint. Susan looked pristine in her white blouse, having opted out of the game. She smiled.

"I learned a long time ago not to get involved."

"But I want to be involved. I want to be part of her life."

Susan looked at her. "Laura, did you enjoy the game?"

"No."

"Then why did you play?"

"I want to be a part of her life, I need to understand the things she likes."

"You *are* a part of her life. You don't have to be involved in everything, you have your own interests, let her have hers. You're trying too hard."

"I have to try hard. She spends so much time with them, I feel like I'm competing. I have to be accepted by the whole world before she can be mine."

"She *is* yours. Chris doesn't bring her girlfriends around, ever. No one else before you. The fact that she brought you here is proof enough that she's crazy about you. They all like you, and you aren't competing with anyone. You've already been accepted. These people are her family, the only family she knows. They mean a lot to her, and she brought you to meet them. Isn't that enough?"

"So, to her this is like taking me home to have dinner with Mom."

"Exactly. She's a firefighter, not a normal person like you and me."

"I don't see what her job has to do with anything."

"That's why you try too hard, because you don't see it. It's not a *job*, it's a *lifestyle*. Firefighters, cops, EMTs, they're different from the rest of us. Do you know that one of the highest rates of divorce in the country is among emergency services personnel?"

Laura furrowed her brow and shook her head.

"Well, it is." Susan leaned on the rail and watched the game. Bryce was on the ground, Chris's blue paint on his face shield, someone else's green paint stained his side. "We'll never understand them. It takes a special kind of person to go into emergency work. They call it a 'Type A Personality.' " She waved her hand, encompassing the entire group below them. "These guys will tell you they got into this business to help people." She shrugged. "Maybe they did, at first. But they stayed for the adrenaline rush. They get addicted to it. Just look at them. When they aren't at work, they're here shooting each other. Or skydiving, bungee jumping, snowboarding, whatever. Anything dangerous, anything for that rush. We don't understand. We try to tame them, keep them home with us. But that just drives them away, usually to someone else."

Laura leaned over the railing, turning her head to look at Susan. "But I would understand if she'd explain it to me. She won't talk to me about work."

"You don't want her to. There are some places inside her you don't want to go. I used to try to get Bryce to talk to me, until he did once." She shivered. "They see things out there every day that no one should see and stay sane. I had nightmares for weeks. Now I send him out for a beer with Shelby, or call Chris."

"Why?"

"Shelby is his partner, she understands where he's coming from. Chris is a Debriefer, she's trained to handle hearing that stuff. *I* can't handle it."

"I think I could, if she'd just talk to me."

Susan turned completely so that she could look fully at Laura. Her voice became earnest. "Don't do that to yourself, Laura. You're sweet, you still have some innocence, don't lose that. Don't ask her about the job."

"Why not? Maybe she shouldn't be coming out here and shooting her friends. Maybe she'd feel better if she talked about it."

"She can talk about the job with *them*, don't ask her to talk to you about it."

Laura turned to Susan. "But I want to know how she feels, what she thinks. I want to be a part of every aspect of her life."

Susan shook her head. "Do you, really? Do you want to trade projectile vomiting stories over pizza and beer? Or find the humor in what looks like a tragic accident to everyone else? Do you want to know what it feels like to work so hard, just to have your patient die? And do you really want her to tell you? She'd be wracked with guilt for years. Don't make her do that to you. Don't make her describe to you what it smells like when blood mixes with gasoline."

Susan saw the blood draining from Laura's face as she spoke, and she leaned closer to drive her words home. "Don't make her relive the horror of watching someone die, screaming in pain, or taking the mangled bodies out of wrecked cars. Don't make her tell you what it's like to carry babies out of buildings, not knowing what color they were before they were burned black."

Susan turned her face back to the game and lowered her voice to a whisper. "Don't do it, it'll ruin your relationship, it'll ruin you. Let her go shoot her friends, dive off cliffs, whatever she needs to do to get that shit out of her head. Don't cage her in. Don't drive yourself crazy." She tipped her head toward the players again. "Tori and Shelby have lasted this long because they're both in it, they get to be crazy together."

Laura was a little breathless. "But you're not in it, and

you've kept Bryce for so long. How do I do that with Chris?"

Susan shook her head and kept her eyes on the game. Chris was down, Tori was aiming at Shelby again. "Just let her have what she needs from the people who understand. She'll give you everything she can, you have to learn how to accept it without pushing for more." She sighed. "There's the old story, the one about the sirens calling the sailors to their deaths. The sailors know they'll die, but they can't resist the sound." She waved her hand below. "They chase sirens, too, only theirs have flashing lights with them. The rest of us don't understand it, but we chase them just like they chase that siren call. But if you take that away from them, they'll die. Inside, they'll die."

"So I have to let her go to keep her."

"You have to learn to hold her without holding on." Susan laughed. "The spouses, they call us emergency widows. Our lovers are still alive, we just hardly ever see them. We usually band together when they go off on their group things. You should get to know some of us; you'll find some support there."

Laura looked doubtful and relieved at the same time. "Really?"

Susan hugged her. "You're one of us now."

Laura's gaze traveled across the room, taking in the latticework, wooden railings, and the small sign above the stage that read "Copacabana Club" and showed the establishment year. She took in the bar, with its rustic overhang and the bamboo shades pulled down over the windows. Lita, short, dark and attractive, gave her a winning smile as she brought a tray of shots to the table. "First one's on me!"

Laura smiled shyly back at her, feeling embarrassed at

the quick pang of jealousy she had felt when the owner of the bar ran up and hugged Chris as soon as they stepped in the door, then blushed as she caught a flash of a tattoo on Lita's chest when she leaned over to set the shots on the table.

Chris leaned close. "Leta and the girls have always been really good to us."

I'll bet everyone's good to you. Laura glanced at the waitresses moving about busily, carrying trays of drinks and emptying ashtrays. Alex was tall and thin, with curves in all the right places, silky fabrics clinging to her body as she moved. Bari was nearly as tall, her face half hidden by a black hat that wasn't quite western, her muscles bulging around the leather she wore. They suddenly deposited their burdens as Kid Rock's "Cowboy" blared from the speakers and met on the dance floor, their blond hair and slim bodies intertwining in a dance of pure sexual energy. Laura watched with growing amazement as the rest of her table hooted and cheered them on, everyone in the bar on their feet to watch. She looked at Chris as the girls kissed each other lightly on the lips and turned back to their work.

"Are they a couple?"

Chris grinned. "No. But they know how to put on one hell of a show, don't they?"

Laura shook her head, speechless.

"Hey, Joe, how'd you get that shiner?"

Laura shifted in her seat to see the man Tori was talking to. Joe, a middle-aged, overweight man with fading bruises around his left eye, was at the other end of the tables they had pushed together to accommodate their group of about twenty-five. He grinned at Tori.

"I didn't use morphine before I zapped a guy."

"Ouch!" Shelby laughed. "He was happy with you, I see."

"Yeah, that's the thanks I get for saving his life!" He stood up and held out his hands. "So there I am, trying to get orders for this guy's chest pain, and suddenly he goes out on me. I look at the monitor and he's in SVT, rate of two-twenty plus. So what do I do?"

Bryce grinned. "Cardiovert!"

Joe slapped the table in front of him. "Damn right! No time for niceties."

Laura looked at Chris, confused. Chris leaned over and spoke in a low voice. "SVT, the heart's beating so fast it's not pushing the blood around the body. You have to shock the heart into a more normal rhythm. Cardiovert. It hurts. Kind of like putting a nine-volt battery to your tongue, only something like ten million times worse."

Laura nodded and turned her attention back to Joe, who was pantomiming thumbing the buttons on his defibrillator. "So we hit him with two hundred joules. He jumps off my cot and hits me with a roundhouse, damn near knocks me off my feet."

The whole table was laughing as Joe swung his fist in a roundhouse, connecting his own fist lightly against his black eye, and stumbled backward. "Then he looks up at me and says, 'You son of a bitch, you hit me again and I'll kill you!' Now I have to walk into the ER with my left eye swelling shut. And Carol here can't even treat me, she's too busy laughing her ass off."

Carol, the young blond ER nurse with glasses, looked at him. "Oh, but you deserved it, after that drunken asshole you brought me earlier that night. He spent two hours in my ER trying to decide whether he wanted to spit on me or grab my ass! I finally had to mask him and tie his hands just to defend my honor."

Joe leaned over the table and looked at Carol. "Like you have any honor left to defend."

Jason, a dispatcher, shook his head. "Stupid people

tricks. I swear, sometimes you just want to strangle them."

The girl next to him turned and asked, "What was your last one, Jason?"

"Which one? God, yesterday I got a hysterical man on the phone who had a cat scratch on his arm!"

"No way!"

"Oh yeah! And nobody knows where the hell they live. I got this call the other day, this woman's in a panic. 'My baby's choking!' I said, 'Ma'am, where are you?' So she says, 'I'm in the living room!' "

"No, she didn't!"

"Yes, she did!"

"And the baby?"

Jason waved his hand. "Baby's fine. Spit up whatever it was while Mom was dialing the phone."

Lita stepped up on the little wooden stage and called out a name Laura didn't recognize. A man from their group got up, went to the stage, and started singing a Garth Brooks song. Chris elbowed Will sitting next to her.

"Hey, Will, you've got to tell these guys about that kid in the staircase."

Will flushed. "Nah, they don't want to hear that."

There was a chorus of "yes we do"s and "come on"s from around the table. Will sighed.

"There's not much to it, really. I was working for this department down South, and we got called out on this stuck kid. We get there, and it's this great big fancy house, must have cost a fortune. The kid's parents are off some-where and the live-in nanny is in a panic. This little boy, maybe two years old, is on the staircase with his head poked through the vertical uprights of the banister." He grinned. "This poor kid is just dripping with cooking oil. I guess he stuck his head in there and when he couldn't get it out, the nanny poured oil all over him, trying to slide him back out. It was the most pitiful sight, this kid sitting there halfway up the stairs with oil just dripping off him; his ears were all red where she'd been trying to pull him backward out of there."

The group at the table laughed. "So, what'd you do?"

"Well, my first instinct was to cut the spindles holding him in, but the nanny had a fit. I guess these people had had this banister shipped in from some foreign country or some shit, and it was worth like a million dollars. Well, the kid had gone through face first, and he couldn't get back out because his ears were catching. So we picked him up and turned him over, and brought him out face first. With all that oil, he slid right out, but it took three of us to hold on to the slippery little guy."

Gary, a young police officer sitting next to Carol, looked at Will. "You didn't have to cut the banister?"

"Nope, just turn him around and slide him through."

"Damn! I'd have cut it just for spite."

"Nah, the nanny was already in a panic. Besides, I wanted to get on her good side. She was beautiful!"

"Oh, so now the truth comes out! You didn't want to save the banister, you wanted to impress the nanny!" Shelby tossed a peanut at him. "Did it work?"

"Yeah, I impressed her, but not enough. She turned me down."

"Aw, poor baby." Chris gave him a look of mock sympathy.

Will batted his eyes at her. "But you could make me feel all better, Elvis."

Laura leaned over and put her arms around Chris, one hand casually falling on her breast. "Not on your life, buddy."

Bryce brought his fist down on the table. "Oh, man, I believe you've just been *told*."

Chris smiled, leaned over and kissed her lover.

The man who had been singing came back to the table and Lita called Diane, another ER nurse, to the stage. She stepped up, and Chris leaned over to Laura.

"You've got to hear this. Diane's awesome."

Laura turned her attention to the stage and the whole table sat in silence as Diane began to sing "Wind Beneath My Wings," softly at first, then raising her voice to an incredible pitch. Laura listened in awe.

"Oh, my God!"

Chris grinned. "Didn't I tell you?"

"And she's a nurse?"

Chris nodded.

"Why? She has so much talent . . . Why?"

"Same reason we're all here. We love what we do."

"But she could go professional!"

Chris nodded. "Yep. And Will here paints like you wouldn't believe. That dispatcher over there," she pointed to a small woman in the middle of the table watching the stage, "she writes. Good stuff. Ryan could have been a model. Bryce drums with a band on the weekends." She shrugged. "But this stuff gets in your blood. Into your soul somehow. God knows it doesn't pay much, but we can't just walk away from it. We just can't."

Laura shook her head as Diane softly closed her song and they all cheered wildly. Lita climbed back onto the stage. "We have a special treat here at the Copacabana Club tonight. Chris, Shelby, come on up here and do your old standby!"

The crowd yelled, but Shelby shook her head and waved them off.

"Oh, no. No, no. I'm not doing it again. Last time nearly killed me!"

"Oh, come on girls! Just once for old time's sake!" Bryce pleaded.

Shelby shook her head. "No way. You guys don't have any idea what that song takes out of me."

"Oh, come on, Partner. You know we all love it."

"Then you do it."

"I'm a drummer, not a singer." Bryce looked over at Chris. "Help me out here, Chris. You can get her up there."

Chris shook her head. "I don't do that song anymore."

"Why not?"

She gazed at Laura. "Because I don't. I've got better things in my life to sing about."

The crowd at the table began to chant. "Meat Loaf! Meat Loaf!"

Laura pushed her lover. "Go on. Go sing for me."

Chris looked at her, then at Shelby. Shelby shrugged. "I'll only go up there if you do."

Chris stood up and held out her hand to Shelby. "Meet?"

Shelby laughed and put her hand in Chris's. "Mrs. Loud."

The tableful of people cheered and whistled as they stepped onto the stage, hand in hand. They each picked up a microphone and began to sing "Paradise by the Dashboard Light." Tori slid into the seat next to Laura, laughing.

"They don't just sing this one, they *do* this song. You've got to see it."

Laura watched for a minute as Shelby and Chris sang and acted out the song. A smile played about her lips as she spoke to Tori without taking her eyes off the stage. "They've been doing this a long time."

"As long as I've known them."

"Were they ever lovers?"

"No, of course . . ." Tori stopped and frowned as she

watched. "Come to think of it, I never asked. They were always friends; I never thought about it. I guess I don't really know."

Laura glanced at her before turning back to the stage. The guys at the table were whistling and calling out to them; Shelby and Chris ignored them. "You really don't know?"

Tori looked up at the stage. Shelby was on her knees, begging Chris to let her sleep on it. "I thought I did. I thought I knew everything about Shelby." She shook her head. "No. They couldn't have been. They're both too . . . ego driven. I don't think they would have been able to stand each other."

Laura smiled as Chris and Shelby began to pray for the end of time. "You're probably right."

"Yeah." Tori returned to her seat as Chris jumped off the stage and Shelby stepped over to speak to Lita. Chris kissed Laura quickly before she sat down.

Shelby set her microphone back into its stand and began to sing "Every Time I Roll the Dice," her smoky voice taking on a whiskey and cigarette quality that the crowd cheered on feverishly. Tori laughed and clapped when she finished. Chris gave her a high five as she went back to her seat, greeted by a kiss from her lover.

Lita stepped forward and beckoned to Chris. Chris took Laura by the hand, led her to a chair in front of the stage and sat her down. She slowly climbed the steps and picked up the microphone. She smiled sweetly and began to sing "A Natural Woman" in a smooth and even tenor as she gazed at Laura.

Shelby and Tori stopped and looked at each other, both of them with their mouths hanging open. Shelby shook her head. "Oh, my God, am I seeing this?"

Tori shook her head. "I don't know, can we both be hallucinating the same thing at once?"

Will leaned over. "I think it's sweet."

Shelby shook her head. "You don't understand. Chris doesn't do sweet."

He shrugged. "It looks like she does now."

Chapter Thirteen

Chris leaned against the outside wall of the fire station in her workout clothes and toweled the sweat from her face. Will walked out the door and stood beside her, sweat showing through his T-shirt.

"You do that workout every day?"

Chris shrugged. "Every day I work."

"Damn, you must be a rock!"

"Just trying to stay fit, you know. I have to be able to pull my own weight around here."

"Chris, you more than pull your own weight. You've proven that you're as good as the men, better than most. Why do you keep trying so hard?"

"I'm not. I just like to stay on top."

He grinned. "Yeah, I'll bet. Hey, I had a great time the other day. I never knew you could sing. You and what's-her-name, Shelly?"

Chris smiled. "Shelby. We've been doing that one a long time." She appraised him carefully. "Maybe longer than you've been alive."

"Oh, not that long, you're not that old!"

She grinned. "Thanks for the sentiment, but I could almost be your mother." *I could almost be Laura's mother. God, am I really doing this?*

"No! How old are you, really?"

Chris gazed across the street, watching people go in and out of the convenience store there. *Wow, how old am I? I don't feel old. Where did all those years go?* "Forty-two this year."

"Wow, your girlfriend's a little young then."

She raised an eyebrow and looked at him. Will held up his hands in a peaceful gesture.

"Not that there's anything wrong with that. I mean, hey, if that's what you want, go for it. I like her, I think she's cool."

Girlfriend! God, is that what she is? It's been so long since anybody's been my girlfriend. It sounds so juvenile. Isn't she something more? She smiled and cuffed him on the head playfully. "Come on, pup. Let's go for round two."

Will groaned and followed her inside.

Shelby leaned up on one elbow and watched Tori lying in bed beside her. She reached out and touched her lover, running her fingers lightly over her skin.

"What are you doing?" Tori spoke without opening her eyes.

"Nothing." Shelby continued to caress her lover.

"You're still doing it." Still, Tori didn't open her eyes.

"I can't sleep."

"Why not?"

Shelby shrugged one shoulder. "Too light?"

Tori opened her eyes and rolled them back in her skull. "Shel, we've only got a couple more nights. I know it's hard, but you've got to try. We can't be tired at work."

Shelby flopped onto her back and sighed. "I know. I just . . . I don't know."

Tori sat up and looked at her. "Okay, what's on your mind?"

"Nothing really." *Everything. What the hell am I doing here? Is this all my life is? Is there more out there?*

"Nothing? Then why can't you sleep?"

"I don't know." Shelby threw an arm over her eyes. "Just got a lot on my mind, I guess."

"Like?"

She sighed. "I don't know. Maybe it's just nights. I hate nights."

Tori turned and slowly began to stroke Shelby's face with her fingertips. Shelby unconsciously tipped her head so that Tori had a better reach. Tori smiled. "So put it all out of your mind. Think about something else."

"Like what?"

"How did you like Chris's girlfriend?"

"Chris's girlfriend. Do you know how weird that sounds?"

"Yes, but we'll get used to it. I like her. I thought she was nice."

"I guess she's all right." Her words came slowly, almost slurred. "It's just weird, you know?"

Tori's voice lowered to a near whisper. "Yeah, I know." She continued to stroke Shelby's face a few moments, and then whispered again, "Shel?"

"Mmm?"

Tori smiled. *Works like a charm, every time.* "Nothing."

Tori lay back down and settled her head on her sleeping lover's breast. Shelby automatically wrapped her arm around her in her sleep.

Laura sat across the table and looked wide-eyed at Hannah. The table between them was full of tarot cards, laid out in a pattern that Laura couldn't quite remember.

"I don't understand."

Hannah touched several cards briefly, bringing her graceful hand to rest on one. "In your environment, the things and people around you, there is trouble. Fighting, illness, destruction. Possibly death."

Laura shook her head. "No. Nothing like that is happening."

Hannah looked at her intensely. "Yes. It is happening. It *will* happen."

"Where? With who?"

Hannah closed her eyes and breathed deeply. She sat motionless, then shook her head and opened her eyes. "I don't know. It's all around you. Not just in one area, everywhere. I can't pinpoint it."

Laura shook her head again. "No, it can't be. I won't believe it. I can't."

"Stop, Laura." Hannah reached across the table and touched her hand. "Stop. You're blocking. Denial is a block, and nothing good can come of it. You have to remain open, or you will not be able to help when the time comes."

Laura's mind echoed back the words Chris had spoken to her that first night they had talked, in the bar. *Trust Hannah, trust that she knows . . . whatever it is that she needs to know.* Laura took a deep breath and brought her mind back to center.

"Okay. Okay. Tell me what to do."

"I can't. You are your own person; you can't be told what to do."

"But you can help me."

"Yes."

"Then help me, Hannah. Teach me."

Shelby and Tori were sitting at the kitchen table when Casey came in, duffel bag over one shoulder.

"The guys are here to give me a ride to the game, Moms. I'll see you in the morning!" He leaned down between them and kissed each one on the cheek. Tori reached around and slapped him on the butt. "Be careful!"

Shelby winked at him as he ran out. "Make a couple baskets for me!"

He waved a hand in response as he disappeared out the door, dodging Sammy and her friend Randy going through from the other direction. Sammy waved at her parents. "We'll be playing out back."

"Hey!" Shelby called after them. "I thought you two were fighting."

Sammy gave her an exasperated look. "Mom! That was weeks ago."

They ran out the back door. Shelby looked at Tori and laughed. "Kids! Forever means somewhere between three hours and three days."

Tori smiled, glancing at her watch. "It's nearly time for me to go. God, I'll be glad to get off these nights."

"Me, too."

"Not like you have to be on them anymore, Boss."

"If I'm going to run with the day shift, I need to run with the night shifts, too. Besides, I might as well work nights the same time you do. Maybe I won't miss you so much."

Tori smiled, but it was a distracted smile. Shelby leaned closer to her.

"Are you okay?"

"Fine. I'm just thinking about this bust tonight."

"The drug thing? That's tonight?"

"If all goes well."

"You'd better be careful!"

"I'm just the uniform backup. Besides, I'm always careful, sweetheart." Tori got up and kissed her lover before going upstairs to finish getting ready.

*   *   *

Chris could hear the roaring of the fire and her own slow breathing as she sucked air from her tank through her mask. The flames licked the ceiling above her like a live thing as she made her way into the next room. She saw a body lying on the floor, face turned down, sprawled out as if the person had been crawling before they collapsed. The person had lost their way in the smoke and darkness, turned wrong and ended up in front of a bookshelf instead of the door. Chris trained her flashlight on the petite body and saw Laura, tousled hair and smoky clothing clinging in the heat. She signaled the guys in her crew, lifted the light body easily, and headed down the stairs. She came out of the burning house and ran to the nearest safe zone. Laying the body down, she rolled it over.

It was a teenage boy, not Laura, but her mind flashed a picture of her lover in front of her eyes. She yanked her mask off and shrugged out of her air tank. She leaned over the boy; he was breathing. The ambulance crew ran over with an oxygen tank and started taking care of him. Chris watched them until they wheeled him away, trying to sort through her confused thoughts.

Chris sat down on the street, dropping her helmet beside her. She pulled off her fire hood and the bandanna that kept her hair in check, and put her face in her hands, rubbing hard, leaving soot streaks on her face. Her captain clapped her on the back. "Your boy was the last one, Chris, good job."

She tipped her head in acknowledgment but didn't respond. She sat watching the rest of her crew as they finished putting out the flames in what was left of the two-story house.

I should be in there helping, the job's not done.

But the image of Laura had left her weak and shaking.

That boy, he was the right size. His hair looked like hers.

She rubbed her face again. Never had thoughts of someone else intruded into her mind like this. She had been inside there, fighting the monster. She had done her job well enough to save someone, but her mind wasn't there. She had to get Laura off her mind, at least at work. She sighed. *I'll talk to Shelby, she'll understand. Later. Now I just want to go home and wrap my arms around Laura. Thank God I'm on short shift.* She got up and started tossing her gear into the truck.

Shelby held out her clipboard for the ER nurse to sign her paperwork. She looked down at the patient she had just brought in, a tiny old woman. *Stroke. No doubt about it. And not her first.* The nurse signed the paperwork and Shelby tucked the clipboard under her arm as the patient groped, catching her hand and clutching it. Shelby reached down and patted the old woman's hand, deftly extracting her hand from the woman's clutch. She smiled as reassuringly as she could, smoothing the wispy hair from the woman's brow and murmuring words of encouragement. The woman stared up toward the ceiling, her cataract-covered eyes not seeing it, and made no response to Shelby's voice. *I doubt she heard me,* Shelby thought as she walked quickly out to her ambulance, *and if she did, she doesn't understand.*

She stopped outside the ambulance and lit a cigarette. Bryce stepped over and looked at her.

"I thought you quit that."

Shelby took a long drag. "I did."

"It looks like it. That shit'll kill you, ya know."

"Bryce, you are neither my mother, nor my wife. So get off my ass, okay?"

"No can do. It's in my contract, right there in small

print at the bottom. 'Must stay on Shelby's ass as much as possible.' God, I love my job!"

Shelby shook her head, but she smiled. Bryce grinned back. "Who's driving, Boss?"

"You."

"Great!" He disappeared around the front of the ambulance. Shelby finished her smoke and climbed into the passenger seat. Bryce was tapping the steering wheel and singing about old time rock and roll with the radio.

Bryce turned the music down and looked at Shelby. "Where to, Boss?"

"Let's stay mobile for a while. I'm feeling restless."

He pulled out of the drive as he laughed at her. "You're worried about Tori."

"I guess." She shrugged as she turned up the scanner. "Maybe it's just the calls. I hate nursing homes. Those people are so . . . helpless." She shook her head. "I can't do anything for them. I need to be out there, doing something important."

"Yeah, like checking up on Tori."

She raked her fingers through her hair. "Something like that. Let's go downtown and get a soda."

Bryce turned toward the convenience store across town that gave them free drinks. "Thank God Cindy's not with us tonight."

Shelby sighed. "I know, I'm just as relieved as you are. I don't know what I'm going to do about her."

"What do you mean? She's not cutting it, get rid of her."

"It's not that simple."

Laura watched Chris lean her head back on the sofa and close her eyes. *Just like the first time she was here. Was it only a few weeks ago? I feel like I've loved her for-*

ever. She smiled at the memory and leaned down to kiss her.

Chris kissed Laura back, and then gazed into Laura's soft brown eyes. "You're bad for me, you know."

Laura furrowed her brow. "Bad for you? From what I hear, you're as bad as they come."

Chris smiled and pulled Laura down on top of her. "You have no idea how bad I can be."

Laura giggled. "I have a pretty good idea! But how am I bad for you?"

Chris sighed and ran her fingers along the line of Laura's jaw. "I can't get you off my mind."

Laura returned Chris's touch, lightly following the bone structure in her lover's face with the tips of her fingers, smoothing her sculpted eyebrows, touching her lips. "And what should we do about that?"

Chris brought her face forward, almost touching her lips to Laura's. "I have to find a way to get you out of my system."

Laura breathed her breath and whispered her own back. "You just need to get enough of me."

"I don't think I can." Chris covered her mouth in a kiss, her hands pulling the small woman tighter to her body.

Tori crouched behind a shrub at the edge of the lawn, glanced toward Ryan and nodded. He ran in closer to the house, staying low, keeping his head down. They could hear the angry voices inside the house and they tensed, waiting for the signal to approach. Suddenly, a shot rang out, and they both sprang into action.

Tori saw the man run out the front door with a gun in his hand. She recognized his face.

Oh, God, it's him! Why didn't we . . .

Then the bullets began to fly.

* * *

Bryce continued the conversation while they filled their drink cups from the soda fountain. "I don't see what the problem is. Just get rid of her."

"I keep hoping . . . you know it takes longer for some to catch on. She's just got so much heart, she really loves this."

Bryce looked at Shelby as they walked up to the register. "I'm not going to tell you how to do your job, Boss, but she's not going to get it."

Shelby glowered at him. "Thanks for your opinion."

Bryce nodded, knowing that the subject was closed. The checkout girl waved them through; they both smiled and thanked her, climbing back in the ambulance. Bryce glanced at Shelby. "Where to?"

She sighed. "I don't care. Just drive."

Bryce nodded and pulled out, turning down a street at random. "So, how are the kids?"

"Oh, they're fine. Casey had a basketball game tonight. Sammy and her friend Randy are playing together again. I guess he's decided it's okay if she likes girls since he likes them, too."

Bryce laughed. "That's the way I see it."

"Me, too."

"How about the other two?"

"I know what you're doing, Bry. You're trying to keep my mind off Tori."

He looked at her with wide, innocent eyes. "Who, me?"

She laughed. "Okay, I'll play your game. Erica's being a loner. She spends all her time in her room since we got her that electric keyboard a couple months ago."

"She always did love music. Just like her Uncle Bry."

"And she's getting pretty good. You'll have to come listen to her."

"I'd love to. I'll have her in the band before long."

"Oh, no you won't. She's not old enough to play in the bars with you."

He shrugged. "The kids have been asking when we're going to see you again. I think my Billy still has a crush on your River. He never stops talking about her."

"She probably likes him more than me right now."

"Bullshit, Shel. River loves you, she's just rebelling right now."

Shelby sighed. "I know. It's a stage, it'll pass. I just think that if I hear 'I don't have to, you're not my mother' one more time . . ."

Tori's voice came over the radio, stopping her in mid-sentence. "Six-oh-three to Dispatch, backup needed, three-three-seven North Fifth, shots fired."

Bryce turned a corner sharply, changing direction, heading toward Fifth Street. A male voice neither of them could identify came over the radio.

"Officer down, requesting backup! Shots fired, officer down! Send an ambulance!"

Shelby flipped on the lights and siren, grabbed the mike and called their dispatch. "EMS Seventeen en route, three-three-seven North Fifth, officer down, possible gunshot."

She snapped the mike back on its holder and put one hand over her mouth, not even hearing Dispatch repeat the information. Bryce glanced at her as his foot pushed harder on the gas pedal.

"Shel? You okay?"

She reached down and started pulling on a pair of gloves. "ETA?"

"It's not her, Shelby. It's someone else, not her."

She jerked her head up and looked at him, her eyes filled with fury and fear. *"How fucking long until we get there?"*

"Four minutes."

"Thank you." She unfastened her seatbelt and climbed through the opening into the back. Her mind raced, going over every possible gunshot injury. *It could be anywhere. Worst case, it's head, anything else can be handled.* Images of Tori intruded; she pushed them back as her hands worked, hanging IVs, setting up the monitor, unlocking the drugs. *Could be more than one, be ready for anything.* She moved around the back of the ambulance, unaware of Bryce's erratic driving. She yanked the pillow and blanket off the stretcher, replacing them with a backboard and straps. *Backboard, no matter what. Could be into a vest, blunt trauma. Bruises, maybe broken ribs. God, who is it?*

"Bry! ETA?"

"One to two!"

Shelby tore several strips of tape, sticking them to the bar above the cot, glanced around to make sure she couldn't do anything else before grabbing the trauma bag and stepping down into the well beside the side door. She opened the door and jumped out almost before Bryce had the unit stopped.

The world looked to Shelby as if it was moving in slow motion. The emergency lights of several police cars and her own ambulance bathed the scene before her in flashes of competing color, making shadows jump and move. She was in the front yard of a small, dirty house. A uniformed figure was lying on the ground near the porch, another uniformed person was kneeling over the first as if in prayer, or some strange healing ritual, with hands pressed against the chest of the injured officer.

Shelby's eyes locked on the two uniforms and she started to run toward them. Another officer stepped out from behind a tree and tackled her. He pinned her against the ground as she struggled to free herself.

"You can't go in there!"

"Shelby!"

She jerked her head up at the sound of Tori's voice calling her name. It was followed by a loud pop. *Gunfire. They're still shooting.* The gunfire sounded far away to Shelby, miles away.

The officer pinning her grabbed for his radio, which was saying something about the suspect heading east on foot. Shelby scrambled to her feet and ran toward Tori's voice.

Tori was on the lawn, just in front of the porch steps, leaning over another officer. Her bloody hands pressed to his chest and shoulder. She was yelling at him.

"Ryan! Ryan, goddamn it! Talk to me, buddy!" She looked up, Shelby saw pain and fear in her eyes. "Shel! It's Ryan, Shel! Ryan!"

Shelby's smoky voice dropped even lower as she knelt beside Ryan and spoke through her teeth. "Tori, get out of here."

Tori jerked her head, reacting to Shelby's words like a slap in the face. The tears threatening to spill from her eyes were suddenly gone. She felt calm. "He took two hits, one to the left shoulder, one to the right chest. Nine millimeter, I think. His respirations are shallow, decreased LOC, he's bleeding out."

Bryce and an officer came running up with the stretcher. Shelby barked at them, her usually calm voice sounding tense and angry. "Get me a bird."

Bryce nodded. "On the way. Landing on the corner."

Shelby's tone didn't change. "Load him, I'll do everything en route."

Tori held her hands in place, pressing on the holes in Ryan's body while Shelby cut off his uniform. Shelby paused for a split second as her shears came to his badge,

closing her eyes. Then she yanked it free, letting the uniform shirt fall off of him as Bryce and the officer rolled
him onto his side. Shelby ran her hands and eyes down
his back, looking for exit wounds. She bandaged the one
she found and motioned Bryce to place the backboard.
They rolled him onto the backboard, strapped him down,
and lifted him to the cot.

Tori ran beside the stretcher, holding pressure on his
wounds while they wheeled him to the ambulance. She let
go as they loaded the stretcher into the ambulance, feeling
tissue bulge out of the wound as her hand left his chest.
"Oh, shit! Bandage!"

Tori jumped aboard with Shelby. Bryce slammed the
doors and ran around to the driver's seat, blaring the siren
as he pulled out. Shelby threw a dressing to Tori and
grabbed the bag-valve-mask. Tori slapped the dressing in
place and took the mask from Shelby, using it to push air
into Ryan's lungs while Shelby slid needles into his arms,
threading catheters into his veins. She pulled the needles
back out and dropped them to hook up the IVs.
"Sharps on the floor!" She called the warning loud
enough for Bryce to hear. His only response was to
pull the ambulance across the intersection of the
streets, positioning the back end as close to the landing
zone as he dared.

Just as Shelby was opening up the valves on the IVs,
Tori began to notice resistance when she tried to squeeze
the bag.

"He's hard, Shel."

Shelby listened to his lungs as Tori squeezed again. She
couldn't hear anything on the right side. She tossed her
stethoscope aside and grabbed another needle. *Second in-
tercostal space, just above the third rib.* She felt for the
space between Ryan's ribs and slid the needle into his chest,

pushing to puncture the inner wall, and heard a sound like air going out of a tire. Tori squeezed again.

"Got it!"

Shelby jerked her head to one side, tossing her sweat-soaked hair out of her eyes as the back doors opened, the flight crew jumping on board. She gave them a quick report as they moved Ryan to the flight stretcher.

"Early twenties male, two entrances, shoulder and chest, possible nine millimeter." She pointed to the bloody bandages, then to a spot near the center of Ryan's chest. "One exit on the back here, bleeding controlled. We decompressed," she waved her hand over the needle sticking out of her friend, "got air return there. Decreased level of consciousness, bagging with his respiratory efforts. Fourteen gauge each arm, AC space, one LR with blood tubing, one NS with a maxi-drip."

The flight nurse nodded as they clicked the last straps in place. "Any history? Allergies? Meds?"

Tori shook her head. "No meds, don't think there's history, unknown allergies."

The nurse nodded again. "Okay, let's go."

Shelby and Tori each grabbed a corner of the small cot, the flight crew took the other corners. They ran to the helicopter, instinctively crouching to avoid the rotating blades, and loaded him aboard.

Shelby and Tori had barely stepped back from the aircraft when the pilot took off, rising straight into the air before turning his copter around and flying toward the hospital.

Shelby dropped to her knees, her bloody hands held up near her chest and tears in her eyes as she watched the blinking lights disappear into the night.

Tori stood several feet behind Shelby, also watching the helicopter. When it was gone, she stepped up behind her. She gritted her teeth, looking down at her lover. "Don't you ever try to order me off a scene again."

Shelby stood up, looking at Tori defiantly. "Don't ever disobey me like that again."

Tori's eyebrows shot up in surprise. "*Disobey?* I am not one of your green EMTs you can order around! And the first thing you taught me was scene safety. You ran in there with blatant disregard for safety. You endangered yourself and your partner."

But you called me! All of Shelby's pain and fear instantly turned to fury. She stepped closer, putting her face in Tori's. "How about a reality check, Tori? You forgot every damn thing I taught you tonight! You put yourself in that situation in the first place!" She pushed against Tori's shoulder. "Where's your vest? That could . . ."

"Reality? Here's reality, that's my partner up there! My *partner!* Fuck the vest! I'm a *cop*, Shelby, that's *what I do*. That's my partner! You would have stayed had it been Bryce!"

"Bryce wouldn't have been stupid enough to be there!"

"Being there is my job!"

"And that could be you up there bleeding!"

"You have no right . . ."

"Hey, hey!" Bryce stepped between them. "You both need to calm down. Standing out here yelling at each other isn't going to help Ryan. We all had one hell of a scare, and we all need to calm down."

Tori and Shelby looked from him to each other. Tori dropped her head and looked at her hands, covered in blood.

"He's my partner, Shel, and my friend. I love him."

Shelby looked at Bryce, who stepped back, giving them some room but still watching. She couldn't imagine the torture within Tori. She couldn't imagine losing Bryce as

Tori had just lost Ryan. "I know you love him." She looked at her own bloody hands, wondering where she had lost her gloves. "I love him, too."

Shelby and Tori stood apart, only touching their foreheads together, each of them silent in their own pain as the tears began to flow. Bryce quietly walked away, letting them calm each other. He watched them as they parted, then slowly walked back toward the ambulance side by side. He waited there with some water, to help them wash away Ryan's blood.

Laura was sleeping soundly when the pager beeped insistently, bringing her out of her slumber. Chris jumped up and grabbed it before Laura was fully awake. Laura watched her as she carefully read the message and picked up the phone, dialing without bothering to turn on a light. She listened intently for a moment, and then said she'd be right there. She hung up the phone and began dressing quickly. Laura sat up and ran a hand through her tousled hair.

"Chris, honey, what's wrong?"

Chris sat on the bed to pull on her boots. "That was the stress management coordinator. There was a shooting tonight, an officer got hit." She pulled the legs of her jeans over the tops of her boots and looked at Laura. "It was Ryan."

"Oh, no. Is he all right?"

"I don't know."

"Can I do anything?"

"No." Chris touched her face. "I don't know how long I'll be, maybe all night. Will you wait for me?"

Laura kissed her. "As long as it takes."

She watched Chris leave and glanced at the indented pillow and rumpled sheets beside her.

Can I stand this? Her jumping up and running out at all hours of the night? Being at everyone's beck and call? Can I share her like that?

Susan's voice echoed in her mind. *They're like sailors, following the siren call.*

Are they, Susan? Or are they the sirens, calling us? Are we the ones sailing to our deaths, trying to catch them?

Chapter Fourteen

Tori stood in front of her locker, thumbing through her ticket book. She studied each ticket, looking for something that would jog her memory.

It's here, I know it is. I know that son of a bitch from somewhere. Please, God, let it be a ticket.

The desk sergeant poked his head in the door. "Hey, Pataki, how's Reid?"

She waved her hand at him. "He's going to be all right. One slug hit a lung, but the doc says he'll make a full recovery."

"That's good, glad to hear it. You been through IA?"

"Yeah."

"That go okay?"

"Sure. No problem."

He started to back out of the room, then pushed the door open and stepped all the way inside. "Pataki?"

Tori looked up at him, irritated. "What?"

"I just wanted you to know that I'm sorry about your partner. The guys here, they give you a lot of shit, and I just wanted you to know it doesn't matter. You're a good cop, we all know that. It probably doesn't mean much . . ."

Tori looked at him. "No, it does. It means a lot, Sergeant. Thanks."

He nodded and backed out of the room. Tori looked at the door a moment, and then finished thumbing through the rest of her tickets.

"Damn it!" She tossed the ticket book back in her locker and slammed her fist against it, thinking. *It was a Mercedes, or maybe a Cadillac, dark, with tinted windows. And he was an asshole. Ryan wanted to search the car. God, why didn't we? He studied us, marking us in his mind. He sneered at us, like he knew we wanted him and couldn't have him. No PC, we couldn't. All we could do was write him. But where's the ticket? Where's the fucking ticket?*

She suddenly looked at Ryan's locker. *I didn't write him, Ryan did. That's why I can't find it, it's in Ryan's book.*

Shelby knelt in the dust and leaned over the man. She glanced up at the construction site four floors above, and frowned, looking back down at her patient. She reached out and took his head, holding it steady, feeling mush where she should have felt bone.

Damn. I can't believe he's still alive.

Bryce leaned over her. "What do we got?"

Shelby shook her head. "He's FUBAR."

"Call it?"

"I can't, he's still breathing. Let's just scoop and run."

Bryce and Shelby quickly rolled the man onto a backboard, putting all their immobilization equipment in place. They lifted the board without waiting for the stretcher and walked quickly to the ambulance. Bryce started to climb in beside her; she shook her head.

"Let's just go. Call in for me, tell them we have a fall of four plus stories, multisystems trauma, open head." She glanced at her gloves, odd looking soft tissue sticking to the blood on them. "Gray matter showing. Light it up, Bry."

Shelby's hands quickly ran over the injured body as the ambulance began to move beneath her feet. *God, he's broken. How the hell do they expect us to fix this? I can't help this guy.*

She yanked off her gore-covered gloves and pulled a clean pair on before placing the sticky patches on the man's chest and turning on her cardiac monitor. She glanced at the rhythm of his heart as she opened her IV start kit and began preparing a site for the needle. *Why is his heartbeat so strong? He should be dead. I can't believe he's still breathing. He's probably too broken to even be a donor.* She threaded the needle into his arm and glanced up to meet Bryce's eyes in the rearview mirror. He had the mike up to his face and she knew he was reporting what she was doing. She nodded once to let him know the IV was in and began securing it with tape.

"We're here," Bryce called to her from the front of the ambulance as he pulled into the hospital drive.

Shelby just had time to secure the cardiac monitor to the cot and lay the IV bag beside his head before Bryce had the unit stopped and the back doors open. She waved at him to go and he pulled the cot out as she jumped out beside it. A nurse met them at the doors and began leading them to a room as Shelby gave her report.

"Fall from four plus stories, I don't have any ID or medical information on him yet. He's got an open head, gray matter showing." She almost laughed. "He's got a sinus rhythm, and respirations of twenty on his own. I managed an IV in the left AC space, fourteen gauge, I don't have a current blood pressure."

The nurse stepped into a room and they wheeled the

cot up beside the bed. She looked at Shelby in amazement. "Why isn't he dead?"

Shelby shook her head as she began to unhook her monitor and help the nurse hook up the hospital equipment. "Your guess is as good as mine. This guy's so broken, I can't figure out why his heart's still beating, much less why he has spontaneous respirations."

"He's a construction worker?"

"I believe so. The scaffolding didn't come down; bystanders said he just fell off."

The nurse shook her head. "Okay. Anything else?"

"Nothing I know. Bryce?" Bryce shook his head. "No. He's all yours then. We'll be back for a signature."

The nurse waved them off, already engrossed in her work, as other hospital personnel began to squeeze into the small room. Shelby stepped out of the room and helped Bryce pull the cot after them and wheel it back to the garage. He began cleaning up the cot and ambulance; she grabbed her clipboard out of the front and stepped outside. She lit a cigarette and sat down on the bucket placed there for a makeshift bench, and looked down at her blank paperwork, seeing instead the broken body of the man she had just brought in, with Ryan's face, then Tori's.

God, I don't think I want to do this anymore. I don't think I can.

Tori leaned down beside Ryan, ticket in hand. "I know who he is, Ryan."

Ryan looked up at her. "What?" He couldn't do any more than whisper.

"Cowlin. Remember the guy we cited for speeding? The one we didn't feel right about?"

Ryan thought hard.

"You know, the tinted windows, gym bag in back, no PC to search?"

Ryan nodded, recognition in his eyes.

Tori held up the ticket. "I got everything I need. I'm going after the son of a bitch. I'll get him, Partner, I promise."

Ryan shook his head. "No," he whispered.

Tori watched his lips. "Yes. He's mine. Shoot my partner. I'll get the son of a bitch."

Ryan shook his head again. "Not alone. Get hurt."

"I won't go alone, but I'm taking him down."

Ryan pulled her close and whispered in her ear, "Careful, love. Careful."

She kissed his cheek softly and smiled at him before she left, tears shining in her eyes.

Shelby pulled up in front of the bar. She noticed the Harley parked near the door and knew it belonged to Chris. As soon as she walked through the doors she saw her friend sitting near the pool table. She bought a beer and went over to sit with her. Chris looked up at her approach.

"So how's business?"

"Okay, I guess. And yours?"

Chris nodded. "Not too bad. So why are we here?"

"I don't know. I guess I just don't know where else to go." She threw up her hands and sighed. "I'm finally off duty, and there's no reason to go home. Pretty sad, huh?"

Chris looked at her seriously. "Only if you look at it that way. Where's Tori?"

"At the hospital." She shrugged. "Or home, either way, she's still at the hospital."

Chris got up, put quarters in the pool table and racked the balls. Shelby methodically picked out a stick. She leaned over to break. "It's just that," she paused while she drew back her stick and shot. The balls scattered, Shelby watched the two roll into the corner pocket. "I've never been there, you know?" She aimed another shot and missed.

"Been where?" Chris aimed for the fifteen and dropped it in the side pocket. She put the twelve in the corner, missed the nine. Shelby leaned over and aimed.

"Been where she is. I've never worked on my partner." She sank the one ball and aimed again. "Seven to three combo in the corner." She made the shot and aimed another, sliding the stick back and forth in her fingers. "I've never thought my lover fucked up on the job." She missed.

Chris took her turn. "And she thinks you fucked up." She made the ten, thirteen, and eleven as she spoke. "Or you think she thinks that?"

Shelby shot, dropped the five, and missed the six. "I don't know, Chris. She won't talk to me. She's so hell-bent on catching the shooter. When she's not working on that, she's at the hospital. When she is home, all she talks about is Ryan, and how she can't wait until he comes back to work." She straightened up and leaned on her stick. "What can I say to that? God, Chris, it could have been her."

Chris leaned over to shoot. "Yes, it could have." She made the nine, aimed at the fourteen. "But it wasn't." She missed her shot.

Shelby looked at her, still leaning on her stick. "And that's supposed to make me feel better?"

"No. But it's something to think about. Your shot."

Shelby glared at her before leaning back over the table. "So, I'm thinking too much about what could have happened." She missed. "And not enough about what did. Is that what you're getting at?"

"Maybe." Chris pocketed the fourteen and took careful aim at the eight ball. "Far corner. Maybe you just need to think about what's really bothering you. Your rack."

Shelby put her quarters in the table and racked up the balls while Chris bought them each another beer. Shelby stood to the side of the table, drinking her beer and watching Chris break. "So, did I?"

Chris shrugged. "Did you what?"

Shelby leaned over the side of the table and aimed. "Fuck up on that scene."

"I don't know, Shel, I wasn't there." She put her palms down on the table and leaned over it, her face inches away from her friend's. "Did you?"

Shelby tossed the hair out of her eyes with a casual jerk of her head. "Nobody's perfect. Everybody makes mistakes. I've fucked up on scenes before."

Chris furrowed her brow. *Why does she want me to think she was wrong?* She brought her fist down on the table and straightened up to her full height. "On *this* scene, Shelby? As a paramedic, *as a supervisor*, as an instructor, *tell me*. Did you fuck up?"

Shelby leaned over, shot, and dropped a ball, aimed again. "No." She looked up through her hair at her friend. "I did not."

Chris nodded. "And I ask you again, does Tori think you did, or do you think she thinks that?"

"Oh, she thinks it all right."

Chris raised an eyebrow and looked up at Shelby sideways from her position at the table.

"I don't know! Maybe it's my imagination."

Chris took her turn, waiting on Shelby to finish changing her mind.

"Okay, so what if you're right? How do I stop wishing she'd quit her job?"

"Would you quit yours for her?"

"That's different."

"*Really.*" Chris drew the word out in mockery.

"EMS is not dangerous."

Chris grinned. "Weren't we in the same EMT class? Did you miss a day? Have you missed the last fifteen, twenty years?"

Shelby couldn't help but return the grin. "Well, it's not *as* dangerous."

Chris rolled her eyes.

"But what do I do now?"

"Nothing. You go home. You hug your better half, and thank God you still have her." Chris reached out and brushed the hair from her friend's face. "You get a fuckin' haircut. You go on. You get over it."

Shelby shook her head, her hair falling back into her eyes. "I can't do that."

Chris cocked her head. "Why, your stylist out of town?"

Shelby rolled her eyes. "No, asshole, the getting over it part. That's what I can't seem to do."

"Why not?"

She threw up her hands. "I don't know. You're the expert, you tell me."

"Okay, I will. You don't want to get over it. You want it to be a big deal. You don't have enough stress in your life and you want more."

Shelby shook her head. "You're wrong."

Chris arched her eyebrow. "Am I? Then why?"

"I don't know."

"Don't know or won't admit?"

Shelby shrugged.

Chris tipped her beer toward her. "Then you're on your own, girlfriend."

Shelby laughed. "That's the best you can do for me? Some friend you turned out to be."

One side of Chris's mouth raised in a quirky smile. "Do you remember Allison?"

Shelby cocked her head to one side and thought. "Allison . . . Allison . . . I think so. You dated her for a while, cute little blonde?" Chris was nodding. Shelby suddenly brightened. "Yeah, I remember her! Whew, what a . . ."

"Yeah, yeah." Chris interrupted her with a wave of her hand. "Do you remember what you told me about her?"

She was nodding. "I told you that I couldn't help you out with her, you had to figure that one out yourself."

"Precisely. Now you have to figure this one out on your own."

"But that was a completely different situation; she wanted you to . . ."

Chris tapped the pool table twice, cutting her off. "Look sharp, my friend, six o'clock."

Shelby turned around to see Tori walking through the door. Chris went to her, hugged her, and then sat down at the bar. Tori walked over to Shelby.

"Hi. Been here long?"

Shelby shrugged. "Couple of beers." She took another drink. "How's Ryan?"

"Good. He's asking about you. You plan on driving home?"

"You going to arrest me?"

"No. Shel, maybe you should come home with me."

"Maybe not." She took another drink.

"What have I done to piss you off?"

"Nothing."

Tori threw up her arms in exasperation. "Come on, Shelby, I thought we passed up 'nothing' years ago. I'm too fucking old to play this bullshit game with you. Talk to me."

Shelby set her beer down hard. "The way you look at me, that's what's wrong. Like it's my fault."

"What?"

"You spend half the night at the hospital with Ryan, then come home and talk about him. You don't say out loud that it's my fault, but your eyes say it all."

"Shelby, you didn't pull that trigger. I'm not accusing you of anything."

"Yes, you are. I didn't get there soon enough, I didn't treat properly, I didn't hyperventilate soon enough. *Fuck.* I don't know." She dropped her head into her hands. "I don't know."

"So that's it. You think I think you screwed up."

Shelby didn't raise her head.

Tori leaned toward her. "Have I ever disagreed with you and not told you?"

Shelby shook her head, feeling miserable and mean.

Tori reached out and touched Shelby's chin, lifting her face to look at her. "You did everything right by Ryan. You saved his life. Yes, you screwed up, but you didn't hurt him. Your only mistake was getting personal. You taught me that you can't get personal on any call. But you did, and so did I. You were scared. Hell, we both were. I don't blame you, I thought you blamed me."

"You? For what?"

"For losing it on that scene. For sounding like I blamed you. I didn't, I don't."

"Oh, no, I never blamed you. I wished I would have fucked up; that would be better than you *thinking* I had. Or thinking that it could have been you. Your job is too dangerous, I don't want you hurt, or killed."

"I'm *not* going to get hurt. My job is no more dangerous than yours."

Shelby opened her mouth to argue, Tori held up a hand to stop her.

"Come on, let me take you home. We'll come back for your car tomorrow."

Shelby closed her eyes. "I'm sorry . . ."

"Hush." Tori wrapped her lover's hands in her own. "Come home with me."

They stood and put their arms around each other. They walked hand in hand, Tori leading Shelby to the door. Chris grinned at them as they passed, her thoughts turning to Laura.

Chapter Fifteen

Tori crouched behind a bush at the edge of the yard. *This is it. Two weeks I've been looking for this son of a bitch, and now he's mine. Shoot my partner, my friend, I'll kill the bastard.* She gripped her gun, her finger unconsciously slipping over the trigger, her eyes glued to the front door of the house in front of her. The SWAT team leader looked at her.

"You ready?"

Tori nodded. "He's mine, don't forget that."

"Pataki, don't make me take you out of this. You're here because I let you come, don't forget that. Don't do anything stupid."

Tori narrowed her eyes to slits and glared at him. "I won't do anything stupid. I just want this guy."

"Of course you do, we all do. Reid is one of our own, we take care of our own. Just don't get carried away with it."

She hid her anger and nodded. "Okay."

The SWAT leader looked at her hard before turning and signaling to his team.

Chris walked into the bookstore and looked around. Hannah smiled at her and pointed. Following her hand, she saw Laura, her back toward her, rearranging books on a shelf. Chris grinned at Hannah and put her finger to her lips as she sneaked up behind Laura. She wrapped her arms around Laura's waist.

Laura smiled and leaned her head back against Chris.

"Hey, you just let anybody come up behind you like that?"

Laura looked up at her from the corner of her eye. "Only you."

Chris breathed in her ear. "And how did you know it was me?"

Laura turned around in her arms and grinned. "Now, you don't really expect me to tell you all of my secrets, do you?"

"Yes."

"Ah, but then I wouldn't be able to keep you intrigued, now would I?"

"Oh, no fear there. You intrigue me, little girl."

"Who are you calling a little girl? Honey, I'll show you things you never dreamed of."

"Really." Chris laughed warmly. "Things you learned where? In a book?"

"You'd be surprised." Laura took Chris's face in her hands and kissed her. Chris closed her eyes and let herself fall into the kiss.

Laura broke the kiss and laughed deep in her chest. "Come over tonight and I'll show you."

Chris shook her head. "I don't want to come over."

"No?"

"No. I want you to come to my place."

Laura stopped and looked at her, wide-eyed. "Your place? No one goes to your place."

"Who says?"

"Oh, come on. Have you ever taken a woman to your place? In say, the last few years or so?"

Chris raised one eyebrow. "No."

"See! It's your sanctuary. It's your safe zone. Nobody goes there."

"Well, maybe you're nobody. Or maybe I don't need a safe zone anymore."

"Maybe you don't."

"When did you figure out all of this stuff about me anyway? Who told you?"

"Nobody. I just know." She glanced toward Hannah.

"Oh, no! Hannah's been rubbing off on you!"

"Not rubbing off, teaching."

"Great, now I'll never be able to hide anything!"

"Do you need to?"

Chris gazed at her and smiled. "No. For the first time in my life, I don't. I'm an open book to you."

"Good, I love to read."

"So you'll come tonight?"

"I wouldn't miss it for the world."

"Great, I'll pick you up at closing time."

Laura raised her eyebrows. "And take me there, helpless without a ride home?"

Chris wiggled her eyebrows suggestively and let her go, stepping back from her. "That's the idea!"

Laura smiled as Chris waved and walked out the door.

The man in handcuffs looked at Tori and sneered. "Officer Pataki."

Tori looked at him, no expression showing on her face. "Mr. Cowlin."

The SWAT leader looked from Tori to the prisoner, back to Tori. "You two know each other?"

Tori stood without moving. "No."

"Of course we do, though not in the biblical sense, unfortunately. But we did meet once, and I never forget a face. Especially one as *pretty*"—he drawled the word

out, making it sound lewd—"as the one on our fine officer here." He turned back to Tori. "So tell me, Officer
Pataki, how is that handsome partner of yours? Was it a
nice funeral?"

Tori made a disgusted sound. "No. You missed. He's
fine."

Tori thought she saw anger flicker across his face before he turned up his poisonous smile. "Well, well, what
do you know? My shooting isn't as good as it used to be.
It'll be better the next time we meet."

Tori turned to the SWAT team around her. "Did all of
you just hear him threaten the life of an officer?" They
nodded. "Thank you, Mr. Cowlin. That'll do just fine."

"Oh, but guns won't be the only thing I shoot next
time we meet, Officer Pretty." He stuck his tongue out in
a gesture that sent a shiver down her spine. She shook her
head and turned away from him.

"Take him. I changed my mind. He's your bust, I don't
want anything to do with it."

Shelby was in the den working on a lesson plan for her
current EMT class when Tori came in with a beer in her
hand. Shelby looked up from her books as Tori threw
herself on the sofa.

"Bad day at work?"

Tori made a disgusted sound. "Bad month." She took
a drink of her beer. "But I got him. That son of a bitch is
gone."

"Hmm." Shelby sounded distracted. "Did you kill him?"

Tori shook her head. "No. I wanted to."

"Well, that's good. I'm glad you caught him."

"Me, too. Now, if I only didn't have to go in tomorrow."

"I thought you loved your job," Shelby taunted.

"I do. I just hate being stuck with the rookie from hell."

"The rookie from hell." Shelby turned her eyes back to her books. "I've got one of those."

"Not like this. She doesn't know anything about being on the street, and won't let me help her learn."

"She sounds like mine." Shelby shook her head. "I thought I could teach anyone, but I'm not so sure now. Little Cindy tries so hard; she's got all the heart I could wish for. But she can't function on the street. Not even Bryce has been able to help her."

Tori scoffed. "At least she doesn't act like you're going to attack her." She made a rude noise. "As if I'd have anything to do with a mousy little bitch like her. I despise weak women."

"No, that seems to be a cop thing; you always get all the homophobes."

"EMS has its share, too. *You* just don't get them as often as *I* do. And you've got Bryce; you don't have to partner with them anymore."

"You don't either, you know."

Tori set her beer down and pressed her fingertips together, trying to control her anger. "Shelby, we've been over this a million times. I can't quit my job."

Shelby began organizing her papers. "Yes, you can. With my promotion, I've got a twenty percent pay increase. And if I pick up another class, the teaching gives me another full-time paycheck fifty weeks out of the year. You could quit."

"And you'd be working all the time. Besides, it's not the money, and you know it. I'd go crazy not working."

"Fine. You're an EMT, I've got an open position."

"Work for you?" She snorted. "No way!"

Shelby tossed her pen in her book and closed it hard.

"And what's so bad about working for me? My employees don't seem too bothered by it."

Tori lifted her beer to her lips. "Of course they don't. They aren't sleeping with you." She took a drink. "Or being protected by you."

Shelby rummaged around in her desk drawer for a cigarette. She found a pack, shook one out and lit it. "Just what do you mean by that?"

"I thought you quit that."

She waved her hand, smoke floating around it. "I did. You're changing the subject."

Tori rolled her eyes and sighed. "I would go *nuts* working for you. You tell me your job isn't dangerous . . ."

"It isn't."

"Yet you'd put me on all the bullshit transfers so there wouldn't be any chance I could get hurt. I couldn't stand you hulking over me every day, being so damn overprotective."

"Hulking?"

"I can't do it, I *won't.*"

"Is it so bad that I don't want you to get killed?"

"I'm not going to! God, just because Ryan got hit doesn't mean I'm next! There's no psycho out there carving my name on a bullet!" *Or is there? I should tell her, but I can't. Not while she's like this.* "Can't you just lay off?"

"No, I can't! Do you have any idea how many cops I've hauled over the years? Ryan just brought it closer to home, that's all. Every time you walk out that door, I wonder if you're coming home alive."

"And I don't wonder that with you?"

"It's not the same."

"Oh, it's not the same *kind* of danger, so it's better." Tori rocked back and forth on the sofa, emphasizing her words, tossing her hands in anger. "*Tell* me, *do* you wear a belt in the back of your rig? When did you *stop* crawling around wrecks? Broken glass, sheared metal, chemicals all *over* the place. The back of your rig is a *cage*, and you crawl into it with every psych patient you pick up. *They* aren't *dangerous*? And how *do* you protect yourself from *every* disease known to man?"

"Hey, I wear my gloves."

"That'll help against TB."

"And I'm careful. I don't have maniacs out there whose only goal in life is to kill cops. *Cops*, not paramedics."

"Unless they think they can get your narcs. You know damn well there are those out there that wouldn't even blink before blowing you away for that box of drugs you carry. You walk into the same scenes I do, and you don't even carry a gun for defense."

Shelby blew out smoke and crushed her cigarette out. "People are not shooting at me on a regular basis."

"And if they do, you don't even have body armor."

"And you don't wear yours!"

"That's my problem, okay? Not yours."

"No, it's *our* problem. Yours, mine, *and* our children's. I know *I* couldn't survive without you, how could *they*?" She gathered her books and shoved them into her bag. She stood up and went to the door, her voice becoming softer. "I love you. I can't come home one day and tell the kids that you got shot. That you got shot and I couldn't save you. I couldn't put you back together."

Shelby walked out the door, not looking back, not hearing Tori's whispered reply.

"But you could."

River stood by the door and watched Shelby leave, then went into the den, finding Tori in tears. She sat down and put her arm around her mother.

"Why are you and Shelby fighting, Mom?"

Tori wiped her eyes and tried to smile. "You heard that, huh?"

"You weren't real quiet."

"I'm sorry."

"That's okay. But why are you fighting?"

"Because she wants me to quit my job, and I don't want to."

"But she said you could get hurt. Like Ryan."

"I'm not going to get hurt, honey."

"But you could."

"I guess I could."

"Is Mom Shelby leaving?"

"Leaving?" *God, she could. I can see it happening.* "What makes you think that?"

"I don't know. You're awful mad at each other."

What would I do if she did? Could I go on? "Do you want her to leave?"

"No."

Yes, I could go on. I wouldn't die, I'd just want to. "Sometimes I wonder."

"You'd find someone else, wouldn't you?"

"Someone else?"

"Yeah, like Ryan?"

Tori looked at her daughter. "You don't like me being gay, do you?"

River squirmed. "Well, kind of. I mean, I love Mom Shelby and all, sometimes I just wish I had a dad, too."

Tori put her arms around her. "Honey, I can't help that your dad doesn't see you. That's his choice, not mine. And not Shelby's."

"Not him! I don't mean him. I mean someone like Ryan. He'd make a good dad."

"I'm sure he would, but it would never work."

"Why not? You said you love him."

"River, honey, I'm gay, and that's not going to change. If Shelby and I split up, I won't find you a dad. I couldn't be with a man. Yes, I love Ryan, but I could never be *in love* with him. Do you understand?"

River shrugged. "I guess so."

Tori touched her daughter's face. "Besides, Ryan's gay, too."

"He is?"

"Yes, he is. You met David."

"Oh."

"Isn't Shelby a good parent? She loves you, you know."

"I know. I really love her, too. I just get mad sometimes. I guess if I can't have a dad, I want her."

"Maybe you should tell her that. She probably needs to hear it now and then."

"Okay. Mom?"

"Yes?"

"If you got hurt at work, could Shelby save you?"

Could she? She smiled. "I'm sure of it."

"Okay." River hugged her mother. Tori thought for a few moments, then got up and began dialing the phone.

Shelby was wrapping up her class lecture when she noticed Chris slip quietly into the room and sit in an empty chair near the door.

"Any more questions?" No one spoke. "All right, guys, that's it. Next class is on shock and bleeding. Read the chapter, know it, be ready for it. If you need anything before then, you've got my work number."

The students gathered their books and headed for the door. Chris went up to the front of the room to help Shelby clean up.

"Hey, Teach." The old joke made them both smile. "I can remember when we were in class together. Now these guys look like kids to me. You got any good ones?"

"A couple." She shrugged. "Nothing like we were, though."

Chris laughed. "We were somethin', weren't we?"

Shelby looked at her friend fondly. "We sure were." She finished gathering her teaching supplies and sat on a desk. "But I don't believe you came by here just to reminisce."

Chris turned a chair around and sat down, straddling the back of it. "No, I didn't. I came to talk to you."

"Why?"

"Tori called."

Shelby got up and began to clean up the last of the equipment. "Oh, so she sent you over here."

"Nobody *sends* me anywhere. She was just worried about you. And I thought you might want to talk."

"I don't need debriefing."

"Good, I don't intend to debrief you. That's not what this is about."

"Then what is this about?"

"It's about two friends who need each other. Come on, I've got a spare helmet. Let's go for a ride."

Chris took Shelby out past the city limits to an old abandoned piece of property, with the burned ruins of a house and an overgrown orchard next to a small brook. Chris dismounted and took off her helmet. She walked to the edge of the brook and sat down, watching the full moon sending thousands of cream-colored sparks off the water. Shelby followed, sitting beside her.

"This place is beautiful!"

"Yep."

"How did you find it?"

Chris smiled. "I own it."

"Since when?"

She looked up at the moon and sighed. "All my life."

Shelby looked at her, incredulous. "We've been friends,

what, since the dawn of time? You never told me about this place."

"I never needed to until now."

"Why now?"

Chris smiled. "Remember when we met, in class? God, we were hardly more than kids."

"Yeah, I remember. We've done some crazy shit, you and me. We've been through a lot."

"And lived to tell tales."

Shelby smiled at her friend, the smile of a sweet memory. "You're my best friend, Chris, for more years than I care to count."

Chris smiled back. "And you're mine. You've always been there for me, whatever I needed. And I've tried to be there for you, too."

Shelby took her hand. "You have."

"I never dreamed we'd be sitting here, this many years down the line, both of us too wrapped up in our own lives to help each other. And I need you now."

"I'm here."

"You first. Tori called me because you two aren't talking."

"Yes we are . . ."

"No, you're not. You're arguing, not talking. Shelby, I love you, but you're being unreasonable."

"I'm not."

"You can't ask Tori to give up her career, she's worked too hard for it."

"No harder than we have ours."

"Bullshit. She's taken more crap than you and I put together. We've been out so long that it's a nonissue for us. We're shocked when someone *doesn't* know we're gay. But she's had to fight every inch of the way. You can't ask her to give that up. Would you give up your career if she didn't like it?"

Shelby shook her head. "I couldn't, you know that. EMS gets in your head, in your blood. You can't just walk away from that."

"I know. That's how Tori feels about Law Enforcement."

"But she's an EMT. She could . . ."

Chris shook her head, stopping Shelby before she finished her sentence. "And you're a firefighter, and I'm an EMT."

Shelby shook her head. "I'm no firefighter."

"You have the training."

"But I can't do that job, and you know it."

"Yeah, I know. And I can't be an EMT. Because we don't *feel* those things. And she doesn't *feel* EMS like you do. She *feels* law. We're cross-trained, but we have to go where our hearts take us. I couldn't give up fire for EMS, she can't give up being a cop for it. Just like you couldn't give it up for fire. She might be good at it, but she doesn't *love* it. You could push her into it, but she'd resent it, and eventually, you. She'd never be happy."

"I couldn't push her into it."

"Yes, you could. You almost have. She's ready to quit for you."

"Well, I'm ready to quit, too. I can't go on this way anymore."

Chris contemplated her a moment. "Are you saying it's over?"

Shelby shook her head. "No. But for the first time I can see the end."

"And that's what you want?"

"No!" She raked her fingers through her hair. "No, I don't want to be without her, without the kids. I just want her to quit."

"She's just about ready to. For you. And you know that it'll kill her if she does."

"It could kill her if she doesn't."

"Would you rather she die doing what she loves, or die slowly inside, day by day, because you won't let her be what she is? You've never been the type of person to repress anyone. Don't start now."

Shelby picked up a handful of pebbles, tossing them one by one into the water, watching the ripples disappear into the current. "I'm scared, Chris. Ryan getting shot just . . . scared the hell out of me. It was too close. Every time the tones go off, I wonder if it's her. I'm afraid to go out on a call. What if she needs me somewhere else, and I'm on another call? I don't think I could function if I had to work on her, and I don't think I could let anyone else."

"I know you, Shelby. You could function. You have a knack for shutting down and running on auto pilot until it's over. You could work on her if you had to."

She shrugged and tossed another pebble. "Maybe. If I don't lose my mind with worry before it ever happens."

"When you worry, when you get scared, call me. We'll work it out together."

Shelby nodded, still unsure, but feeling better.

"River heard you arguing today."

Shelby caught her breath. "Oh my God."

"She's afraid you're going to leave."

"And she's been so angry with me lately. God, I didn't know."

"It's okay, Tori talked to her. But she needs you, too. When you go home, you need to reassure her. She really does love you, you know. Even when she doesn't want to admit it."

"I know."

They sat in silence for a few long moments, Chris trying to get her mind around her own thoughts, Shelby looking around her.

"So, tell me about this place."

Chris sighed. "Am I ready for this?"

"You must be, you brought me here."

"I guess I did. What did I tell you about my mother?"

"That she died when you were small."

"Remember looking for jobs after class? I suggested here and you came with me."

"Sure, how could I forget? I thought you threw a dart at a map and that's where we headed."

"Not quite. I picked this town because of this place. I was ten when we moved away from here." She stood up and looked over the old ruins. "The house was there. It was just after my tenth birthday. Dad woke me up one night and carried me outside. I remember going through the smoke, the fire. It had already spread throughout the house by the time he woke up. Mom was supposed to be right behind us. I stood right there," she pointed at a lone tree standing a few yards from where the house wall must have been, "in my nightgown, waiting for her to come out. She never did."

Shelby could almost see her, such a young girl, standing in the night, fire shining on her skin, wind blowing ashes and hair around her face. "God, Chris, I never knew."

Chris didn't seem to hear her. "I heard the firemen talking. *Fully engulfed.* That's the first time I ever heard that term. Fully engulfed."

"That's why you became a firefighter."

She shrugged. "Probably. Dad didn't want to stay here, but he couldn't bear the thought of selling the place. He signed it over to me and we moved. I grew up. I met you, we needed a place to go, and I figured this was as good as any other."

"Why didn't you ever tell me?"

"I never needed to. Until now."

"Why now?"

"Because I want to rebuild out here. With Laura. I want to tell her, but I needed to run it by you first."

"You really do love her."

"I know, it sounds crazy. We're so different. She's so young . . ."

"Does she care about the age difference?"

Chris shook her head. "She says age is all in your mind. But it's *fifteen* years, Shel. That's a lot."

Shelby shrugged. "That depends on how you look at it."

Chris rubbed a hand across her face. "God, Shelby, I can't get her out of my head. I get intrusive images all the time. I see her everywhere, even on the job. I might be obsessed."

"You aren't obsessed. Just in love."

"But the intrusive thoughts, the images . . . I can't get rid of them. Maybe *I* need debriefing."

Shelby laughed. "No, you don't. The images, the thoughts, they'll be there for a while. Just when you think you're going nuts, you learn to push them back. They don't completely go away, but you learn. You've really never been in love before, have you?"

"Nothing like this." She shook her head. "You know I've never rushed into anything in my life, but I feel like I've known her forever. She's not like anyone I've ever met. She's so put together, you know? She wants me, but she doesn't *need* me, need to own me. She's so sweet, and intelligent. She's *real*. I think I'd die for her. I think I'd die without her. It doesn't make sense."

"Oh, yes it does." Shelby smiled. "That's exactly what I felt when I met Tori, remember?"

"I remember. You were ready to settle down, I thought you were nuts."

"Ten years, and I love her even more, if that's possible. Now who's nuts?"

"Ten years. Now I feel old."

"You are. Some woman having a midlife crisis, riding a motorcycle, with a girlfriend half your age."

They laughed together, before falling into the comfortable silence of friendship, leaning on each other and watching the sun rise.

Chapter Sixteen

Shelby went home and found Tori getting ready for work. Tori glared at her in the mirror as she tucked her hair up neatly.

"I don't even want to know where you've been."

Shelby flashed a smile, a real smile; Tori hadn't seen one like it since before Ryan was shot. "Tori, honey, you've got nothing to worry about. I was out with Chris most of the night, and then I went to see Ryan. He's being released today."

"Really? I thought his doctor wanted him in for a couple more days."

"He told me this morning they're cutting him loose this afternoon."

"Good. But just because you bring me good news, don't think you're off the hook. You stayed out all night and didn't even call. I'm not going to stand for this, Shelby."

"Honey, I was with Chris."

"Oh, so the fact that you were with a beautiful woman is supposed to make me feel better?" Tori tried to keep the smile off her face. Shelby was acting like herself, and Tori couldn't stay mad at her, even if she was worried about her and Chris, which she wasn't. "I don't think so."

"Maybe this will make you feel better." Shelby took Tori in her arms and kissed her. Tori wrapped her arms around her, and her body melted into her lover's. The Shelby she knew and loved was here, really *here*. She hadn't been in so long, and she'd missed her. Shelby lifted her and laid her on the bed.

"Shel, I don't have time . . ."

"Shh," Shelby placed one finger on Tori's lips. Her own lips found Tori's neck and began nibbling. She kept moving down, her fingers caressing, barely touching Tori's body, her mouth working to a rhythm of its own.

Tori tangled Shelby's hair around her fingers, all arguments gone from her mind. She was lost in Shelby's touch, her feel, her lover pleasing her with no thought to her own pleasure.

Shelby brought her to orgasm quickly, enjoying the way Tori whimpered, the strength of her fingers in her hair. When she was sure Tori was finished, she kissed her way back up to her face, seeing the warm glow of satisfaction.

"There, don't you feel better?"

"Sometimes you're a shit, you know?"

"Yes, I am, but you love me."

"God only knows why." She glanced at the bedside clock. "Damn it! I'm late! Shel, I've got to go."

Shelby rolled off her and watched her jump up, rushing to clean up and get her uniform on. "I love you, Tori. There's so much I need to tell you. I've been such an asshole about your job . . ."

Tori reached down and touched her face. "I love you, too. We'll talk about it after work, okay?"

Shelby sighed. She really wanted to tell her not to quit her job, that Chris had talked some sense into her. Tori was rushing, trying to get her hair back up, her uniform on. Her mind already on the job. She watched her snap on her utility belt and lean down for a kiss. Shelby kissed her.

"Okay, after work then."

Tori tossed her a grin as she headed out the door. "It's a date!"

Shelby listened to her go down the stairs and out the front door before taking a shower and getting ready for her own day.

Chris opened her door to find Laura waiting for her. She smiled, surprised and pleased by her presence. "I'm glad you're here. I think we need to talk."

Laura held up a hand, stopping Chris in her tracks. "I'm not sure we do. Where have you been all night?"

"Out with Shelby. She . . ."

"Shelby, of course. Does Tori know about it?"

"I guess she'll be finding out right about now. What the hell are you so mad about?"

Laura looked incredulous. "What am I so mad about? You spend all night out with her, you jump every time she calls, and just leave me here to wait." She shook her head. "I'm trying to give you your space, Chris, I really am. But I have to know. Are you sleeping with her?"

"What?"

"Are you sleeping with her?"

Chris laughed. "With Shelby? You might as well ask me if I'm sleeping with my sister! No, Laura, I am not sleeping with Shelby." She shook her head. "Shelby and I have been friends half our lives. Yes, I do jump every time she needs me, and I always will. Last night though, *I* needed *her*. I took her out to my property last night to talk to her about you."

"Me?"

Chris went to her and took her arms in her hands.

"Yes, you. Look, I've had a rather colorful past, but I've never felt this way before. I needed to talk to Shelby, I wanted to show her where I want to build our house. Ours, yours and mine."

Laura's mouth dropped open and she closed it with a snap. "*Our* house? What are you talking about?"

Chris led her to the sofa, sitting them both down at an angle so that she could look at her, and took Laura's hands in hers. "I was going to take you out there today and tell you about it. I own fifty acres outside the city limits. I took Shelby out there last night to tell her I want to rebuild the house; I want to build it for us, you and me."

"Rebuild?" She shook her head, confused.

"I lived there when I was little. It's kind of a long story; I'd rather tell you out there." She rubbed her face. "Laura, I've loved before, but I've never felt like this. You make me feel . . . I don't know, confused and clear all at the same time. I needed to talk to Shelby last night, to be sure."

Laura tucked an unruly strand of hair behind one ear. "Sure of what?"

"That you're the one. I've never felt this way, I didn't know. Now I'm sure. I know that you're the one I want to share that with. I talked it over with Shelby because I knew she'd understand. She's my best friend in the world, but you are my world." Chris gave her an earnest look. "I'm not sleeping with Shelby, or anyone else. You're the only one I want, Laura. I'll do anything to convince you of that, and to convince you to stay with me. Forever. I love you."

Laura smiled, tracing the arch of her lover's eyebrow with one finger. "I'm convinced."

Shelby walked into the ambulance base just before noon. Bryce looked up from his task of helping Cindy clean a

suction unit she wasn't familiar with. He glanced point-
edly at his watch and winked, Shelby smiled back. Other
crew members were there, hanging around, cooking lunch,
going over the new protocols. One of the guys called out
to her.

"Hey, Boss! We got barbecue ready to hit the table.
There's plenty, why don't you join us?"

"Sure!" Shelby called back. "I never turn down a free
meal! I'll be there soon. Bryce, I need to borrow Cindy a
moment."

Bryce looked at her in surprise, and then noticed the
look on her face. Cindy looked at him, worried. He nudged
her. "It's okay, she won't bite."

Cindy got up and timidly followed Shelby into her office. Shelby closed the door behind her and sat down at
her desk. She leaned over and rested her chin on one hand,
watching Cindy squirm slightly in her seat.

"So, Cindy, how's it going?"

Cindy shrugged. "Okay, I guess."

"You remember those other options we talked about
the other day?"

"Yes."

Shelby sat back and laced her fingers together. "I've
talked to a few people about you, Cindy, and for the
most part, they like what they see in you. They see the
same things I see. You have skills that are important to
this job. But you have some weak points that I can't seem
to figure a way around. But you have so many good points,
and that's why I have given you more time than I usually
would. And I'm willing to give you even more. I just
want you to think about those other options."

Cindy nodded. "Okay."

"I've talked to the ER, and to Cappy in Dispatch.
They're willing to take you on for a few shifts, let you try
things out, see if you like it."

Cindy nodded again, looking crestfallen. "I understand."

Shelby wasn't finished. "My suggestion is that you spend some time in the ER, follow the tech around a couple of shifts, and watch the clerk. And I want you to go into Dispatch a few times, see what they do. I'll schedule you for it."

"If you think that's best. I guess I'll gather my things."

"Oh, no. I'm not firing you, or forcing you out. I just want you to check out your options. Keep an open mind. Will you do that for me?"

"Okay, I can do that."

"And you might like it. I'll schedule you, okay? Make it on the same days you were on this schedule. And I'm not completely taking you off here, just taking you down to a day a week, so you can try these other things."

Her eyes lit up with hope. "You're not getting rid of me?"

"No. Just opening a few doors."

Cindy let out her breath. "Okay."

Shelby unlaced her fingers and tapped them on the desk. "Now, I believe we've got a meal waiting for us."

Cindy smiled. "I think we do."

They both stood up and Shelby squeezed her arm as she opened the door for her. They walked out as everyone else was sitting down at the table. Bryce threw Shelby a questioning glance and she winked at him.

As they chatted over lunch, Shelby was feeling out the crews, finding out if they were pleased with her work so far. She considered all of their suggestions seriously, making sure she was being the kind of boss that she would want to work for. The oldest paramedic, Fred, was explaining his new proposal on tracking statistics when the pager cut him short with a series of tones followed by the dispatcher's voice.

"EMS Twelve, priority one, three-seven-two Madison, elderly female, unresponsive."

Cindy and her partner, Bob, jumped up to go. When he jumped, Bob dropped his fork of barbecue, cursing as it landed on the front of his shirt. Shelby stood up, tossing her napkin on her plate.

"Go get cleaned up, Bob, I'll take it." Shelby called over her shoulder as she followed Cindy out the garage door. She jumped in the unit and Cindy pulled out of the bay. Shelby flipped on the emergency lights and the siren wailed as they sped down the street. The address was only a few blocks from the station, the opposite direction of the hospital. Shelby barely had time to pull on a pair of gloves, toss another pair into Cindy's lap, and gather her thoughts before they were pulling up on scene. She radioed Dispatch and grabbed her medical bag as she stepped out of the ambulance.

A distraught elderly man met them at the door. "It's my wife, please hurry."

Shelby and Cindy followed him to another room and found a woman slumped over in a chair. Shelby knelt beside her, glancing down her body for any obvious signs of trauma, and picking up her wrist, felt for a pulse.

"What happened?"

The man hovered worriedly behind her. "She was just sitting there, and she went out. Is she going to be all right?"

Shelby didn't feel a pulse. She straightened the woman's head to a more natural position. The woman wasn't breathing. Shelby nodded at Cindy. "Code," she said softly. Then louder, as she and Cindy began to move the woman onto the floor. "Sir, what's her name?"

"Erma." He fretted, hovering more closely behind her. "Oh, Lord, she isn't gone, is she? Oh, Lord, no."

Shelby handed Cindy the bag-valve-mask and told her to start CPR while she put cardiac monitor patches on the woman and snapped the wires to them. She clicked a blade onto her laryngoscope and lay belly-down on the floor, leaning her face over the woman's head.

She noticed the color of her skin, the dusky blue of her fingernails, the way her eyes were beginning to look glassy and lifeless.

The man was wailing now, begging her to save his wife. She felt with every fiber of her being that her efforts were futile, even as she positioned the laryngoscope in the woman's throat and slid a tube into place. She listened to her lungs as Cindy ventilated and taped the tube to Erma's face.

The man was leaning over Shelby's back, clutching her shoulders. She did her job, not hearing her own words as she tried to calm the man, tried to get him to step back. She looked up as his hands came off of her, relief washing over her as she saw Tori and another officer, a short, stocky woman with an angry look on her face, pulling him back. They brought the cot and backboard in with them, and the other officer was pulling the man into another room.

Shelby, Cindy, and Tori lifted Erma to the cot, strapped her down, and headed for the ambulance, Cindy compressing her chest as they wheeled her out.

Tori climbed in the ambulance with Shelby, helping her set up IVs and stow away the equipment while Cindy did CPR. When Tori had done all she could, she turned to Shelby.

"Anything else?"

Shelby shook her head. "Not here." She tipped her chin toward the house. "Talk to him for me, I didn't get any information on her. Cindy, let's rock and roll."

Cindy crawled through the opening into the driver's

seat as Tori jumped out the back doors, shutting them and slapping them twice to signal all clear. Cindy took off toward the hospital.

Shelby took over CPR, feeling the ambulance start to move beneath her feet. She worked quickly, adding cardiac drugs to her CPR. She jerked her head, clearing the hair from her eyes and glanced at the monitor, seeing ventricular fibrillation in the readout window. She grabbed the defibrillator paddles and charged the machine.

"Easy, Cindy, I'm going to shock!"

She placed the paddles as she felt the floor steady beneath her feet and thumbed the buttons. Erma's body jumped, Shelby watched the monitor. It showed her a straight, flat line, just as she expected. She pursed her lips and sighed, knowing that the movement she had seen was due to the drugs. *It's playtime now, Shelby, all of it by the book. She's gone.* She placed her hands back on the sunken spot on the woman's chest and began compressing again.

Somewhere, her mind identified the sound of the horn. *That's the stoplight, we're seven minutes out. I need to get a radio report started. But first I need to* . . . the floor lurched beneath her feet as Cindy slammed on the brakes. Shelby instinctively raised a hand to the bar on the ceiling, catching herself before she fell. She tried to get her legs under her, and heard her partner scream.

Shelby heard a loud crash, followed by the tires squealing in protest at the sudden change of direction, and was thrown to the side. She lost her grip on the bar and flew over her patient, crumpling against the wall.

Shelby's world narrowed to uncontrolled movement and sudden mind and body jolting impacts as the top-heavy ambulance rolled, throwing her against each side of the box she was in. It finally stopped, though Shelby didn't feel it, coming to rest on its hood and top front part of the box, windshield shattered on the ground, the siren giving one last sickly wail before shutting down. Shelby's body landing, at last, with a sick thud that no one heard.

Chapter Seventeen

Tori was in her cruiser, two blocks away from the light when she heard the squeal of tires followed by a crash. Traffic came to an immediate halt. She swung the car onto the shoulder and flipped on the lights. She went four car lengths before she saw the accident. Her heart felt like it was caught in a vise, crushing and sinking inside her chest. She gripped the steering wheel and stepped on the gas.

She pulled into the intersection, oblivious to the glass, shredded plastic, and bits of metal crunching under her tires. She slammed the gearshift into park and jumped out before her seatbelt could fully retract out of her way. She could already hear more sirens as other emergency vehicles screamed toward her. She ignored them, and everything else. Her eyes locked onto the demolished ambulance, her mind numb and her feet flying as she ran around it, looking for a way in. She ran to the back doors and couldn't reach the handles. She took her nightstick out of its loop on her utility belt and punched the window with it. It took two more hits before finally shattering, raining glass down on her. She peered inside.

Shelby was lying facedown on the ceiling, beneath the rubble of equipment. The monitor lay across her legs at an angle, incessantly beeping a warning to all that the leads were off the patient. The trauma bag was on her back, and the medical bay lying beside her head, its contents strewn everywhere. Tori could see blood, it looked like a lot to her. She was trying to climb through the broken window when someone grabbed her from behind.

"Tori, no! It's not stable!"

Bryce's words didn't register in her numb mind. "Shelby's in there! I have to get her out!" She tried to wriggle out of his grasp. "Damn it, Bryce, let me go!"

Bryce tightened his grip on her. "It's not stable! You climb through that window and this thing's gonna rock! You'll hurt her more!"

Tori stopped struggling and felt a part of her mind detach from the rest of her, bringing a dreamlike calm to her thoughts. "Okay, what are we going to do?"

"Rescue is stabilizing the unit. I'm going to lift you up so you can reach the handles. If we can open the doors we can get her out faster than cutting through."

Tori nodded and took a deep breath. Bryce made a step with his hands and she placed her foot in it. He lifted her while she steadied herself on the ambulance. She reached the door handle and tugged on it. It opened.

She leaned back to swing the door open all the way, then stretched to reach the other door latch. She caught hold of it and pulled down. The latch clicked open and she tugged. The door wouldn't budge.

"Shit! Let me down!"

Bryce lowered her down. When her feet were back on the ground, she and Bryce grabbed the top of the door and pulled together. They could hear the pop and grind of metal giving way as the door slowly came open. Bryce looked inside.

"Oh, God."

Shelby was still lying facedown, the blood pool beneath her had grown. One of Cindy's arms was hanging down through the opening, unmoving. The cot was still latched to the floor, with the patient strapped to it, arms and hair hanging down, reaching for Shelby like some zombie in a horror movie. Bryce and Tori could hear the groaning metal of the cot latch and knew it wouldn't hold much longer. If it snapped with Shelby under it, she'd be crushed.

Tori stepped into the ambulance and waded through the debris to Shelby. She wanted more than anything to pick her up and hold her; her arms ached for it. Instead, she leaned down and felt for a pulse.

"She's alive! Bryce, she's alive!" Tori began clearing equipment off Shelby, tossing it to the side with abandon. Bryce and another paramedic joined her, clearing everything from the prone body. Bryce tossed the monitor to the side, stopping its beeping. He pulled out his trauma shears and began cutting Shelby's uniform. He went up one leg to her waist, cutting through her belt, continuing up her back to her collar. He went back down her other leg, exposing her completely, running his hands quickly over her body, looking for injuries. Finding none, he laid a backboard on top of her. Bryce, Tori, and the other paramedic turned her over onto the board.

The front of Shelby's uniform looked as if it was soaked in blood. A small, strangled sound escaped from Bryce as he finished pulling her clothes off. He searched frantically for the source of blood while his partner strapped her to the board and Tori held her hand, talking to her. He found cuts on her face and blood coming from her nose. Bryce looked at Tori as she smoothed matted hair back from Shelby's face, and shook his head.

"I can't find a source for this much blood." He shook out a sheet over her exposed body, and then crouched at her head, getting a grip on the backboard. With a nod from his partner, they lifted her and carried her out to a waiting stretcher.

As soon as they carried Shelby out, another crew went in to get her patient. Four people held the cot in place while a fifth beat on the latch, trying to get the cot down with the woman on it. Tori glanced at them as if they were a strange apparition in a dream. Other people were at the front of the ambulance, still trying to get Cindy out, and still more were with the driver of the pickup truck. Tori saw them briefly, moving around her, but she couldn't tear herself from her lover. She couldn't hear the shouts of the rescue workers, or the equipment being used all around her. She whispered to Shelby as she held her hand, begging her to be all right. She climbed in the ambulance with her, staying beside her, oblivious to the paramedic working around her.

Tori realized they were at the hospital when the back doors opened and Bryce began pulling the stretcher out. She walked beside Shelby until they burst through the last set of doors leading to the trauma room, where a nurse stopped her and pointed her toward a waiting room. She stood staring, watching through the small windows, hearing the murmur of voices on the other side as they worked on Shelby. She had never felt so helpless. All she could do was watch, tears streaming silently down her face. She watched. She prayed.

Chris was laughing as she led Laura through her apartment door. She stopped as the door closed and kissed her, lifting her off her feet.

"Marry me, Laura."

Laura giggled, feeling drunk in her joy. "As soon as you're ready, lover."

Chris kissed her again. "Let's start making plans right

away. I want to call Shelby and ask her to stand up with me."

She went to the phone, wiggling her eyebrows at Laura. "It'll be beautiful, you'll see." She noticed the message light flashing and pushed it. "We'll have . . ." She stopped short and the color drained from her face as Tori's voice came through the answering machine speaker.

"Chris, are you there? Pick up, I need to talk to you." There was a short pause. "Um, look, I'm at the hospital. I need you here, Shelby's been in an accident. I don't know . . ." Tears jumped into Chris's eyes as Tori's voice cracked. "I don't know if she'll make it. Hurry, Chris."

Laura put her arms around her lover. "Honey?"

Chris turned around, buried her head in Laura's shoulder, and cried.

Chris and Laura found Tori in the surgery waiting room. Her hair was coming out of its braid in wisps, her shoulders slumped in defeat, and her eyes were red and swollen in her pale, haggard face. Chris hugged her.

"Hey, hon, how is she?"

Tori shrugged, eyes tearing over again. "I don't know. She's in surgery now. They're setting a femur, and might have to relieve cranial pressure." She rubbed her face and patted the pockets of her uniform. "Cigarette?"

Chris shook her head. "Sorry, I quit. Come on, we'll find one."

They made their way down to the emergency room. Chris found a nurse she knew and bummed a couple cigarettes from her. They went outside and Tori held one with a shaking hand while Chris lit it for her. Chris let her take a long drag and cough before she spoke.

"Tell me what happened."

Tori took another drag and tried to get her thoughts in

order. "The ambulance wrecked, she wasn't even supposed to be there." She shook her head. "She wasn't supposed to be there, it wasn't her call. She went because some paramedic spilled barbecue sauce on his shirt." Tori leaned against the wall and slowly sank until she was sitting, elbows propped on her knees, fingers finding her hair, and began to laugh, almost hysterically. "God, barbecue sauce, can you believe it?"

Tori rubbed her face again. "It was a code, I was there. I helped her load up. They got to the stoplight, you know, the one just this side of the base. Some drunk kid heard the sirens and panicked. He hit them in the intersection, they flipped."

"She was loose in the back?"

Tori nodded.

"Bryce?"

"No. It wasn't her call, Chris. She shouldn't have been there!"

Laura handed Tori a tissue and Chris knelt beside her and put her arm around her.

"You were there?"

Tori flipped her cigarette away and nodded again before covering her face with her hands. "I got there just after. I couldn't get her out, Chris. God, I tried, and I couldn't get her out." The last sentence was a muffled choke.

Chris lifted her friend's face and looked into her eyes. "I know you tried. I'm sure you did everything you could. I know you did."

Tori buried her head in her friend's shoulder and cried. Chris held her while she sobbed, exchanging sad looks with Laura. She leaned her head on Tori's.

"Tell me about her injuries."

"Everything was thrown everywhere. When we got in, most of it was on top of her. Everything, the drug box, the monitor, the jump kits, *everything*." She ran a hand through her hair, making more of it come loose. "She's got a head injury. They don't know how bad yet. They said if she makes it through surgery, and if she wakes up . . ." She choked, closed her eyes and tried again. "If she wakes up, she'll make it."

Chris pulled her to her feet and held her. Laura put her arms around both of them, giving them as much support as she could muster. Chris whispered to Tori, "She'll make it. Shelby's a fighter. She'll make it."

Chapter Eighteen

Whispered voices . . .
Whispered voices in her dreams . . .

She concentrated, trying to hear them, make sense of their words. She strained.

"Miss Pataki, we're doing everything we can. It could take several days . . ."

"Will she be . . ."

"We don't know yet . . ."

"Mommy? Mom . . ."

Crying . . . who's crying?

"Come back to me, baby. Come back to us."

She knew the voice, if she could only place it. She concentrated.

"Baby . . ."

Tori! That's Tori! Does she know I'm here? I have to tell her.

She strained to open her eyes. A lance of pain shot through her head. Everything evaporated.

Whispers . . .
Why are they whispering?

"Chris, honey, she's going to be okay. You know that, you told me."

Who? Shelby tried to speak, tried to scream. *Who's going to be okay?*

"Mom, I love you . . ."

River? What's wrong with your mom? Where is she?

Small hands, touching her face, clutching her hands.

"Shel, we're all here . . ."

Bryce's voice, he sounds so sad . . .

Crying, the kids crying . . .

"Mommy . . ."

Oh, God, it's me! I'm the one they're talking about! I'm here! I'm okay! God, help me tell them!

"Okay, guys. Go on home, I'll bet she's tired."

Tired, yes. So tired. How did I get so tired?

Shelby slowly opened her eyes. Even with the lights dim, everything looked so bright. The brightness hurt her eyes, she squinted.

So much white, why so much white?

She let her eyes grow accustomed to the light before she tried to look around. She was in a hospital bed, there was an IV in her left hand and she could hear the steady beep of a heart monitor. Tori sat beside her with her head on the bed, her face almost as pale as the white sheets. Her loose hair spread over her face in wisps, looking like midnight against the whiteness of everything else. She was asleep.

She must be so tired. She never could sleep sitting up. And there are dark circles under her eyes. Poor thing, how'd she get so tired?

Shelby reached over and touched her hair, smoothing it back from her pale, wan face.

God, was she always this beautiful? She must have been. Did I notice?

Tori lifted her head and gave her a strained, tired smile.

"Hey. I've been waiting for you to wake up. How do you feel?"

Shelby groaned. "Like I've been run over."

"I'll bet you do. Do you want a drink?"

She nodded, her mouth suddenly feeling as dry as dust. Tori reached for a cup of water and brought the straw to Shelby's lips. She sucked a tiny bit of the water in and swallowed. "Where are we?"

"The hospital. You had an accident."

"Accident? You're okay?"

Tori smiled and took her hand. "I am now."

"The kids . . ."

Tori shook her head. "No, honey. The accident was at work. We weren't in it, just you."

Shelby closed her eyes tightly and thought. *Spinning, the whole world spinning . . . Her body crashing against the side of the box, the top, the side again, and . . . nothing.* She opened her eyes again.

"Bryce? Where's Bryce?"

Tori reached up and brushed the hair out of her eyes. "Bryce is fine, he wasn't there."

Shelby's eyebrows pushed together in concentration. "No, he wasn't. It was a code, you were there. You and . . . Cindy?"

Tori's smile became a grin. *She's here, all of her! Thank you, God, thank you.* "Yes, Cindy. And I was on scene with you."

"So where's Cindy?"

"She's okay. We were more worried about you."

"What happened?"

"You were in a wreck."

"I remember that, most of it. But after . . . I'm blank."

"You should be. You've been out for a while."

"How long?"

Tori hesitated. "Want another drink?"

Shelby nodded. Tori lifted the straw to Shelby's lips. She took a small sip.

"How long?"

Tori set the cup down and wiped Shelby's lips with a soft tissue. "Well, the accident was six days ago."

"Six days! Why am I still here? How's Cindy, and my patient?"

Tori took her hand and held it. "Slow down. One at a time okay?"

Shelby nodded and took a deep breath. "Tell me."

Tori shook her head. "Your patient didn't make it. But you knew she wouldn't. You told me that on scene."

Shelby watched her and waited. Tori took a breath.

"Cindy's okay, she broke both legs and some ribs, they sent her home already. You were the worst."

Shelby tried to sit up, tried to see herself.

"Don't." Tori pushed her back down. "You broke your leg, cut up your face."

"My face?" She felt the bandages there, one covering her entire left cheek, one on her forehead. "How bad?"

Tori shook her head. "I haven't seen it since it was stitched, but the doctor assures me that if there's any scarring it can be fixed."

"Okay."

"And you fractured your skull."

She reached up and felt her head. "Is that all?"

"Isn't that enough? You damn near didn't make it, Shelby. They were considering opening your head to relieve pressure. You've been unconscious for *six days*. You scared the hell out of me."

Shelby settled down. *Tired, I'm so tired.* "I'm sorry, baby. You've been here the whole time?"

"Most of it. Chris, Ryan, and Bryce have been working in shifts. They make sure someone's with the kids, taking care of them."

"Oh God, the kids."

"They've been to see you every day. They're okay, mostly, considering. Except Erica, she's a wreck. Ryan and David are taking care of them now."

"And who's taking care of you?"

"Whoever isn't with the kids. Right now it's Chris and Laura. And everybody's been by. A bunch of your students came in yesterday, then the whole ambulance crew. They just about drove the nurses crazy; they frown on that many people in ICU at once."

"I'm in Intensive Care?"

"Yeah. It was bad, Shel, real bad."

"I'm sorry."

Tori kissed her hand, smiling through the tears shining in her eyes. "It's okay now. They said if you woke up everything would be fine."

"*If?*"

Tori nodded.

Shelby sighed, trying to get her mind around everything she'd been told. Struggling to concentrate and stay on track. "What about the other car? Somebody hit us."

Tori sounded like she was giving a radio report. "Twenty-year-old male, drunk. Thirteen outstanding traffic violations, including two DUIs. He heard the siren and panicked."

Shelby pursed her lips and her brow furrowed with worry. "Lawsuit pending."

"Not much of one. You've got eighteen eyewitnesses that say he ran the red, and a high BAL. He was drunk."

Shelby sighed and touched Tori's face as her eyes slowly closed again. "You're always looking out for me."

Tori's eyes filled with tears as she watched her fall asleep. "Always."

Chris knocked softly on the door and opened it. Shelby grinned at her and waved her in. She entered, followed by Laura.

"Hey, woman, it's about time you woke up. We've been waiting for you. How was your little nap?"

Shelby rolled her eyes. "I don't remember, I was asleep. You didn't have to wait for me."

Laura spoke up. "Yes we did. I plan to marry this big lug, and she won't do it without you."

"Marriage? I never thought I'd see the day! I wish you the best of luck, Laura; you'll need it to put up with her."

Laura grinned. "I'll manage. You know, we've been spending a lot of time with your kids the past few days. Maybe I'll even talk her into having one of our own someday."

Shelby laughed. "*That* I'll have to see to believe!" She looked around the room. "I want to see them."

Chris patted her hand. "Ryan and David are on their way with them now. But I think you need to see your lady first."

Chris and Laura hugged Shelby and left the room, letting Tori in on their way out. She sat on the edge of the bed and picked up her lover's hand.

"I need to talk to you, Shel."

"Me first. Tori, I've been a jerk about your job. I was trying to tell you the other morning, before the accident . . ."

Tori began to cry. "No, you haven't been a jerk. I never realized how much you worry about me, until I had to worry about you. I don't ever want to put you through that again. I'll quit the force, Shelby. I'll do anything it takes. I almost lost you, I can't bear to go through that again."

Shelby struggled to lean forward. "Oh, no. No, honey. That's what I wanted to talk about. I don't want you to quit. I was a jerk. I was selfish and mean. I know how much your job means to you now. I can't ask you to quit, I won't ever again."

"You're sure? Because I'll quit, I will. I don't care about it anymore, not as much . . ."

Shelby put a finger to her lips. "Hush. I'm sure. I know how much you love it, I won't ask you to give it up. But I will ask for one thing."

"Anything, just name it."

"Wear your vest. Not just on the bad stuff, every day. It was so hard to pick up Ryan, I don't think I could stand to pick you up."

"Okay, okay." She sighed. "I'll wear it. But you have to admit, your job can be just as dangerous as mine."

"Maybe . . ."

"See, I told you so."

". . . sometimes."

They laughed together.

"Shel?"

"Yeah?"

"We make a pretty good team, you and I."

"Yes ma'am, we do. And we always will."

"Always?"

Am I sure? Not too long ago I wondered. She smiled. "Always."

Chapter Nineteen

Tori drove Shelby to the ambulance base. She pulled up as close to the door as she could, even though Shelby was getting around very well on her crutches.

"Are you sure you're ready for this?"

Shelby smiled and winked at her. "It's just an office day. I'll be fine."

"Are you sure I can't help you? I could carry your briefcase, get the door, something."

"Tori, honey, I need to do this. I'll be fine, really."

Tori looked at her face. The puffiness and most of the bruising was gone. And the cuts would heal in time. She reached out and ran her finger lightly along the cut across her lover's right cheek. It ran from the top of her ear down to almost the corner of her mouth. The scar would be thin, almost nonexistent, but she would always see it. She knew she would see it even if it was gone, like a quiet reminder of how close she had come to losing her love. Shelby looked back at her.

"It'll look better when it heals, I promise. And if it bothers you, I'll get it fixed."

"No," she said softly. "Don't fix it." She smiled. "It gives you character. Kind of rugged, like something from an old western. I think I kind of like it."

Shelby shrugged. "Okay, it makes no difference to me. Hey, I need to get in there. There's a lot of work to do, you know. And you're going to be late if we sit here much longer."

"I could take the day off, stay here with you . . ."

Shelby shook her head. "I want you to go get the bad guy. That's what you do. Besides, Ryan would never forgive you for sticking him with the rookie from hell."

Tori smiled. "I know. I'll pick you up after work. I love you."

"I love you, too." Shelby climbed out of the car and hobbled back a few steps, stopping to watch as her lover drove away.

Bryce opened the door for Shelby. She made her way inside, finding all of the employees there, clapping and cheering. Cindy was there, too, in a wheelchair. Shelby went to her.

"How are you?"

"I'm doing pretty well. I've been training in Dispatch, at least until I'm all healed up. I don't know if I want to go back to the field again or not, I kind of like being on the other side of the radio."

"So, it's not so bad, huh?"

She grinned sheepishly. "No, I think I like it better."

"Well, if you decide to come back, there will be a place for you here. At least as long as I'm around."

"Thanks, I really appreciate it."

Bryce pulled up a chair for Shelby. "Sit down, Cindy's got something for you."

Shelby sat down and Cindy blushed a little. "We all got together when we heard you were coming back and got you a little something."

Bryce handed Cindy a box, she in turn handed it to Shelby. She thanked them all and opened it. Inside the box was a card they had all signed and a paperweight, almost the size of Shelby's hand, shaped and painted exactly like one of their ambulances. Shelby felt tears well up in her eyes when she read the one-word inscription on the base: SURVIVOR.

Epilogue

Laura sat at a picnic table in the gathering twilight and watched. She hadn't been pleased with the idea when Chris had asked her to come. The Emergency Conference had sounded like a couple of long boring days for her while Chris was attending classes with other emergency workers. But Chris had promised nights of parties, and a cabin in the woods with a hot tub. And she had delivered.

Now the conference was almost over. This was the last night they'd be spending here. Laura was almost sorry to leave. She had spent her days with the wives and husbands of Chris's coworkers, and the nights with Chris and their friends. And no one had brought a two-way radio, or even a scanner. There was no radio traffic from Dispatch; hardly anyone had even brought a personal pager. It was bliss for Laura.

They were ending the conference with a bash. A DJ had been hired, and almost everyone was drinking and having a good time. Laura was watching Chris.

She was out in the middle of the clearing they were using for a dance floor with her friends. Shelby's cast was off and her scars fading. Tori had one arm around her, the other around Ryan. They were all dancing and singing along to the music. David sat down beside her and shook his head.

"I don't get it."

Laura didn't take her eyes off the dance floor. Chris was laughing, her head thrown back.

Laura smiled. *She's beautiful.* "You don't get what?"

He nodded his head in the direction she was looking. "Them. You'd think they never saw each other. Ryan spends more time with Tori than he does with me."

Laura glanced at Susan, sitting a table down from her. She smiled at Susan and a memory, turning her eyes back to the group on the floor. They were dancing around a little, but mostly singing along to an Alanis Morissette song.

"They're a breed apart, David. We'll never understand them, they're different from us. They're Sirens, and we hear their call. We're attracted to them for their fire, their energy, and then we try to tame it out of them." She shook her head. "We can't do it, and if we could, we wouldn't like what they'd become. It takes a special kind of person to do what they do. And it takes a special kind of person to hold them, one who's willing to sacrifice almost as much as they do, and will give them the freedom to chase after that damn siren call."

"I just want more of him, you know? What can I do?"

Laura smiled, watching the objects of their affection as a gentle summer breeze touched her face, riffling her hair and carrying their voices to her more clearly. Those voices got noticeably louder as they lifted their drinks and toasted each other, singing along with Bonnie Raitt, something about a siren call.

Laura smiled at them. David thought it looked like a smile from a sweet, faraway memory. "Take what he'll give you, David, and be there for him. Don't push him, he'll come around. Love him for who he is, and know that he loves you back. Just love him."

David nodded and looked back at the group on the floor as the music died down. They raised their heads in unison and turned as, in the distance, a lone siren warbled off into the night.